Anna Kavan

Anna Kavan, née Helen Woods, was born in Cannes in 1901 and spent her childhood in Europe, the USA and Great Britain. Her life was haunted by her rich, glamorous mother, beside whom her father remains an indistinct figure. Twice married and divorced, she began writing while living with her first husband in Burma and was initially published under her married name of Helen Ferguson. Her early writing consisted of somewhat eccentric 'Home Counties' novels, but everything changed after her second marriage collapsed. In the wake of this, she suffered the first of many nervous breakdowns and was confined to a clinic in Switzerland. She emerged from her incarceration with a new name – Anna Kavan, the protagonist of her 1930 novel *Let Me Alone* – an outwardly different persona and a new literary style. She suffered periodic bouts of mental illness and long-term drug addiction – she had become addicted to heroin in the 1920s and continued to use it throughout her life – and these facets of her life feature prominently in her work. She destroyed almost all of her personal correspondence and most of her diaries, therefore ensuring that she achieved her ambition to become 'one of the world's best-kept secrets'. She died in 1968 of heart failure, soon after the publication of her most celebrated work, the novel *Ice*.

D1252165

2008   2008

APR   APR

By the same author

Asylum Piece
A Bright Green Field (stories)
Change the Name
A Charmed Circle
Eagles' Nest
I Am Lazarus (stories)
Ice
Julia and the Bazooka (stories)
Let Me Alone
Mercury
My Soul in China (novella and stories)
The Parson
A Scarcity of Love
Sleep Has His House
A Stranger Still
Who Are You?

Guilty

Anna Kavan

*With an introduction
by Jennifer Sturm*

PETER OWEN
London and Chester Springs, PA, USA

PETER OWEN PUBLISHERS
73 Kenway Road, London SW5 0RE

Peter Owen books are distributed in the USA by
Dufour Editions Inc., Chester Springs, PA 19425-0007

First published 2007 by Peter Owen Publishers

© Estate of Anna Kavan 2007
Introduction © Jennifer Sturm 2007

All correspondence quoted in the Introduction is held by the
Alexander Turnbull Library, Wellington, New Zealand
(MS-Papers-7938-05)
© Estate of Anna Kavan, 2007
Reproduced by permission of David Higham Associates

All Rights Reserved.
No part of this publication may be reproduced in any form or by any
means without the written permission of the publishers.

ISBN 978 0 7206 1287 5

Printed in the Uk by CPI Bookmarque, Croydon, CR0 4TD

Introduction

It is possible that around six decades or more have passed since Anna Kavan wrote *Guilty*. Each of those decades has produced unimagined change: social, political, literary and technological advances challenging existing thinking and creating new paradigms. It is so remarkable, then, that this previously unpublished work from Kavan's pen maintains a freshness and immediacy that resonates in the twenty-first century. In the course of transferring ownership of her unpublished work, an anonymous reader inserted an observation between the pages of *Guilty*, indicating an estimated temporal context. The handwritten note, signed 'M.W.' and dated 1989, reads 'this novel is set in the First World War and is related by a youth whose father is a pacifist'.

Kavan was no stranger to war, surviving the First World War as a teenager and losing her only son, Bryan Ferguson, in 1944 to the carnage of the Second World War. She spent twenty-two months, in 1941–2, living in New Zealand with an expatriate English pacifist and conscientious objector, Ian Hamilton. With him she shared the social disapproval and condemnation experienced by those who chose to take such a stance, enduring the receipt of poison-pen letters, always anonymously authored, the whispers of locals and the wholesale dismissal of 'shirkers' by conscripted men and women. It was only when Hamilton's incarceration became an inevitability that Kavan reluctantly, and with considerable difficulty, secured a return passage to England, undertaking an astonishing journey through the enemy-submarine-infested waters of the Pacific and Atlantic oceans, the sole woman aboard a small, battered, wool-carrying cargo ship. It would not be an exaggeration to propose that few other women, of any nationality, would have made the same 12,000-mile voyage during such dangerous times. The ten-week passage provided Kavan with ample time to reflect on the nature of conscientious objection and its impact on her own life. Provocatively, Hamilton's young son, Duncan, was sent to boarding-school during the period of his father's resistance to compulsory conscription. An autobiographical historicity was established, providing a compelling argument that facts preceded fiction.

Before her time in New Zealand Kavan had spent three months in 1940–41 in in New York, assimilated into that city's tight circle of exiled writers, poets, musicians and artists who had fled Hitler's Third Reich and who were referred to as 'Communazis' by FBI boss J. Edgar Hoover. Counting Lion Feuchtwanger among her friends, Kavan was a ready sympathizer with the dispossessed and the 'out-landish', sharing their justified sense of persecution and apprehension. It is therefore tempting to correct M.W.'s estimation and date the setting, if not writing, of *Guilty* to somewhere in the mid-1940s, a possibility that would acknowledge her experiences as a personal and powerful means of informing the narrative. Indeed, the opening sentence of the book tells us that the protagonist's father 'served with distinction in two wars and emerged from the army a minor hero', information that implies participation in the two world wars.

Kavan returned to England on 28 January 1943 after three and a half years away. The culture shock of immediate and unavoidable immersion into London's wartime difficulties profoundly affected her, prompting depression and an urgent wish to return to the relative tranquillity and comfort of New Zealand. Within days of her arrival, she initiated the paperwork required to secure an exit permit and a passage on any vessel bound for the South Pacific. For the duration of the war she continued a regular and, at times, desperately worded correspondence with Ian Hamilton, reinforcing in every letter her regret at having left New Zealand. Her letters illustrate the effect of the impersonal 'machinery' of bureaucracy on the mentality of the individual, whose sole intent might be to house or feed oneself. The following excerpts exemplify the personal experiences which may well have informed the writing of this book.

February 14 1943, c/- Barclay's Bank, Piccadilly Circus, W1
[written while Kavan stayed in a hotel in London]
To find a flat seems quite impossible & I'm still in this place that's full of worldly gilt & decayed past magnificence & American officers with blondes . . . Dolphin Square and all the other big blocks of flats have mile-long waiting lists. The only alternative is some dingy, grim, grey, Bayswater bedsittingroom. I suppose I'll come to it in time.

February 25 1943, c/- Barclay's Bank, Piccadilly Circus, W1
I can't get a flat anywhere, & it's utterly hopeless to find any place at less than 6 guineas, and that's hard enough. Next week I'm taking a large room in Hampstead which is the best I can do. It's probably a mistake, like all my moves, but I have to go somewhere cheaper & that's all I can find.

March 7 1943, 15 Cannon Place NW3
I wish I cd describe these vast government institutions to you: the passes, forms, official documents of all kinds;

the miles of corridors; the innumerable officials to be interviewed [by] in their different bureaux; the extra-ordinarily complicated & apparently irrelevant procedures. It's pure Kafka, of course. At times when I am in one or another of these enormous buildings waiting for an interview with some new authority, I feel as if I were the victim of a private madness induced by too much reading of the 'The Trial' and 'The Castle'.

October 12 1943, Crossways Cottage, Well Rd NW3
I sent a cable to you to tell you that the Authorities had actually granted my permit to leave the country. But of course that doesn't mean that I'll get away soon. All shipping arrangements here are made through a central board & one is simply notified that there's a passage about 24 hours before the ship's due to sail. NZ House informs me that there won't be any accommodation for some months; almost certainly not this year . . . the Authorities may decide to cancel the permit in their capricious & unpredictable way.

Guilty is an anomaly. Deceptively, it resembles in tone and style Kavan's early work, written under her married name, Helen Ferguson, and famously described by her friend Rhys Davies as 'Home Counties novels'. Her occasional use of clichés and the chronological linearity of this story, completely absent in her later work, contradict the Kafkaesque sinister content, leaving the reader unprepared for the disconcerting developments that unfold. It is *Eagle's Nest* (published by Peter Owen in 1957) which the Kavan enthusiast associates most with the work of Franz Kafka. In 1983 Robert Hauptman observed that 'it is in *Eagle's Nest* that the full influence of Kafka and modernism are palpable for the first time' in Kavan's writing (*A Critical*

Survey of Long Fiction, edited by Frank Northen Magill, Salem Press, Pasadena, 1983). Impressed by the 'insistence upon dream, fantasy, and escape into unreality, the quest, the narrative structure, and the ambiguity', he concludes that *Eagle's Nest* 'is one of Kavan's outstanding books, particularly as it is flawless'. I suggest that *Guilty* is more unnerving, more disorienting, and therefore more Kafkaesque, because it adheres more closely to perceived reality, to the ordinariness of a single unspectacular life. No castles, no ruins, no mountainous terrain. The topiary chessmen at Mark's school, ominous in the dark, are, after all, simply trees.

The horror evolves in the simple task of finding somewhere to live in an increasingly unfamiliar world. If the reader of Kavan's impressive list of publications should be called upon to identify an especially 'Kavanesque' feature of her post-1940 writing, he or she would undoubtedly point to the disturbing motif of unreality and to her portrayal of the precariousness of the liminal mindscape between sanity and insanity. The human condition is universal, but few dare to write of it with such acuity. Kavan was a heroin addict and, like her antecedents Thomas de Quincey and Jean Cocteau, she allowed her drug use to take her imagination into scenes denied the non-drug user. Her most successful novel, *Ice* (1967), was chosen by Brian Aldiss as his Science Fiction Book of the Year, an indication of the outer limits Kavan visited in her imagined and imaginary discourse.

While *Guilty* manifests little of the heroin-influenced style or content of Kavan's post-war writing, it does feature several of her recurrent themes. It is no surprise that Kavan chooses 'Mr Spector' as the name of the duplicitous and threatening character who looms over the young male protagonist, Mark. The layered meaning of 'spectre' as both ominous presence and reflected image would have suited her well. The mirror followed her, observing her from all angles and challenging her troubled sense of identity. She was a slave to its critical eye, alternating between self-love and self-loathing but always aware of its spectral and unforgiving presence. Mark is a marked man – his destiny is predetermined and beyond his control, his vulnerability established by the pacifist actions of his father. His inherited boyhood guilt, thrust upon him by social prejudices and compounded by an inability to find acceptance among his peers, primes him for the paranoiac events of adulthood. He becomes 'part of an elaborate hoax, of which [he] was to be the victim'. His weakness is his love for Carla, an emotion that exposes his detachment from his own reality, the 'disconcerting sense of estrangement from [his] own self'.

The British writer and journalist Virginia Ironside, a professed fan of Kavan's writing, has commented on what she identifies in her work as an abiding sense of guilt and associated pending punishment. Ironside speculates on the possible source of this guilt, considering Kavan's heroin addiction and a childish sense of responsibility for her father's suicide. He drowned in the harbour at Tuxpan, Veracruz, Mexico, on 22 February 1911, when Kavan was nearly ten years old. This tragedy had a huge impact on the child, compounding her already developed sense of parental abandonment. Did she experience guilt? Possibly. Children personalize rejection, assuming that their behaviour has somehow causally contributed to the event. However, if Kavan's personal guilt is identifiable, it is to be found in her chosen position of social isolation, a stance necessitated by her impatience with hypocrisy and her intolerance of those she regarded as her intellectual inferiors. Her friends were few, mostly male and often homosexual, and she was wont to estrange herself from them for periods of time, before cautiously reconciling. Mark describes this:

Anybody who's ever attempted to do it will know that it's never easy to start life again, especially with very little money and without friends. Eternal regret is the price I must pay for the idyllic companionship I have known and lost. Now I'm more alone than I've ever been, not only because I no longer have any friends but because I know that however closely another life may impinge on mine ultimately I exist in impenetrable isolation.

The reader of this, the latest in Anna Kavan's impressive list of published works, will be intrigued by her handling of internalized and subconscious guilt. Her ability to navigate the inner landscape does not fail to impress.

Jennifer Sturm
University of Auckland, New Zealand, 2007

Guilty

My father served with distinction in two wars and emerged from the army a minor hero; whereupon he astounded everybody by a public declaration of pacifism. I was very young at the time, but I distinctly remember the day he came back to our country cottage looking most resplendent, I thought, in his fine uniform.

My mother had been to the station to meet him, but I, because I was getting over some childish complaint, had, to my disgust, been left at home with the maid, a disappointment for which I expected compensation in the form of much attention from him. But he only said, 'Hullo, Mark', and gave me a careless sort of hug as he passed on his way upstairs. I was still convalescent and easily upset by small things or by nothing at all and, feeling most injured, began to whimper, glancing at my mother, who, with a flushed unhappy face, was gazing after him. I'd had her to myself for most of my life, and no doubt she had spoiled me, especially during my recent illness. So when she said sharply, 'Oh, don't start grizzling', and then ran upstairs without taking any more notice of me, I was so astonished that I stopped crying at once.

The bang of the back door told me the maid had gone out, hurrying after her freedom, delayed on my account, leaving only the three of us in the cottage. Though I was tempted to creep up the stairs to listen to what my parents were saying, I didn't dare do so with my mother in her present mood, eavesdropping being a sin she condemned severely. All sorts of wild fancies went through my head, of which I favoured most the idea that my father had suddenly gone mad. Perhaps because the voices upstairs seemed to be arguing, my thoughts turned to a sensational crime (lurid details of which I had heard from the servant girl) committed recently by a soldier who, on his return from the war, had slaughtered his entire family.

Suppose my father were to kill my mother and then come down and kill me? My skin crept with delicious horror as I pictured him with the still smoking revolver in his hand, levelling it at me, saying something extraordinary before he fired. Would it hurt much? Would he shoot himself immediately afterwards, or wait to fire the remaining shots at the policemen who would come for him, reserving only the final bullet for his own death?

I still had a shamefully babyish fear of loud noises, and what I really dreaded most was the bang. Our home was far from any town, and treats such as visits to the circus or pantomime were made more attractive by their rarity, but my pleasure was always much reduced on these occasions if a gun appeared on the stage, keeping me in such agonizing suspense that when it was fired at last I could hardly stop myself screaming.

It was a different matter, however, to listen for a shot I knew would never come; an experience half agreeable, half terrifying, like the fearful thrill of the game where you hide in the dark and wait for someone to find you. But my imagination soon proved too strong for me. The pretence was threatening to turn into a waking nightmare, beyond my control, when, to my vast relief, my parents came downstairs again, and I ran to meet them. A sudden sense of something wrong stopped me dead, and I realized they were still too absorbed in their argument even to be aware of my presence – a state of affairs so unprecedented and altogether unnatural that I felt the obscure threat of nightmare again, all the more frightening for being imposed on the surroundings and apparently normal circumstances of everyday.

While the situation oscillated between the two poles of nightmare and norm, I observed that my father, in this short time, had already changed into civilian clothes, in which I did not think he looked half so fine. I recognized the tweed suit as the one that had been hanging up in the big wardrobe ever since he'd left, taken out at regular intervals by my mother, religiously brushed and aired. Despite these attentions, it seemed to me old and shabby compared with the magnificent uniform he had been wearing and was carrying now on his arm. I noticed that he was also carrying several small boxes that looked interesting, as if they might contain presents, and, normality getting the upper hand, I moved forward again.

But nightmare reassumed its ascendancy as he walked straight past as if I had not been there and, closely pursued by my mother, went into the kitchen, thus completing my utter confusion, for I had never seen him in there and hardly thought he knew such a place existed. Should I follow? I had not been told not to. I could tell by their voices that my parents had been caught by one of those sudden emotional storms, always liable to sweep upon grown-up people like typhoons, out of nowhere, strange, frightening, incomprehensible outbursts of love or hate, which seemed to fling them about helpless as battered pieces of wreckage, while I was left out, ignored.

My one small satisfaction was to know I could watch without being noticed; but I had no sooner entered the kitchen than I'd have given anything to have stayed in the other room. Had it been possible I'd have run away. But now, in true nightmare fashion, I was frozen in immobility, unable to speak or move, forced to witness my own horrific imaginings made real.

I'd imagined my father mad, and what but madness could now make him snatch the lid off the dustbin (my voice frozen within me, I trembled all over at the thunderous nerve-shattering clang with which it crashed to the floor) and proceed to stuff his beautiful uniform into it, on top of potato peelings, tea leaves and garbage of all descriptions? The bin was already half full. It was not easy to thrust the garments into it; he had to cram them down with both hands, finally setting his foot on the top of the lot, and with evident satisfaction stamping the fine material deep into the squelching, malodorous mess.

Aghast, I looked at my mother, wordlessly imploring her to stop this madness, or at least to assure me these acts were not as mad as they seemed, appealing to her (as hitherto in every crisis I'd appealed successfully) to save me from this fantastic nightmare. For the first time in my life the assurance wasn't forthcoming. She neither put an end to the grotesque and frightful scene nor removed me from it. And as I watched her fluttering around, pecking and plucking at him with ineffectual darting motions and thin protesting cries, as flimsy and useless as a bird's, it gradually dawned on me that, at this moment, she was almost as helpless as I was myself. She was not, as I'd always believed, infallible and omnipotent where I was concerned; there were some situations against which she was powerless to protect me.

I know one doesn't grow out of babyhood on a single occasion, but I must have taken a long step forward when I made this shocking discovery. And perhaps the peculiar nightmare quality of the episode has stayed so clear in my memory, with all its crazy detail, because it obscured to some extent the realization that the being upon whom I'd lived till then in total dependence was, after all, only human. Meanwhile, it was the turn of the little boxes which had looked so promising, when viewed as I normally viewed the chance of a present. Throughout my father's performance, they had been lying disregarded on the dresser beside me. I wished I'd slipped one of them into my pocket, as I easily could have done at any moment up to now, when he gathered them up in his strong sunburned hands, snapped them open one after the other, ripped out the medals embedded within and consigned these, too, to the dustbin.

I remember our kitchen as rather a dull little room, a drab background across which the decorations flashed, briefly exotic as a shower of meteors, before they slid out of sight with no more fuss and less noise than coins sliding into a purse; far too pretty, I thought, with their rainbow ribbons, to be swallowed by the sordid, dirty grey bin full of disgusting rubbish. Since there was no room left in it for the cases that had contained them, my father threw these on to the floor and dispatched them in the same summary fashion, stamping them into shapelessness and grinding beneath his heel those that resisted destruction.

It was all over in a moment. The glittering discs and crosses were gone without trace. Nothing was left of that brave display but a few broken scraps of framework and torn shreds of leather and velvet, which he kicked into a corner where they could not be seen. Lifting the fallen lid, he replaced it carefully on the bin, looking around to make sure he'd left no sign of disorder anywhere. Then, satisfied that the room was restored precisely to its original state, he went across to the sink and turned on the tap.

A child's time is different from an adult's, and I seemed to have been locked in nightmare for an eternity. I felt I'd reached the ultimate point of endurance where I must escape or die. Most opportunely, the noise of water rushing out of the tap, that most ordinary of household sounds, came now to the rescue, reasserting the existence of all that was known and familiar in my daily life.

The exotic, the splendid, the terrifying, the mad had disappeared, snapped back as if on an elastic band to the world of magic, both good and bad, which for me was all the while lying as close behind the common face of appearances. The sight of my father in his old clothes, calmly and thoroughly washing his hands with green Puritan soap, as if he'd never been a hero or fought in a war, reaffirmed the unreality of the magical. Could I have imagined the uniform and the medals? Could I possibly have imagined the whole incident?

It didn't seem so very unlikely, for there was not then any hard-and-fast line of division between my two worlds, which at times overlapped in a confusing manner. I thought of the tall, thin man, as substantial as my parents in every detail of his appearance and just as much a reality to me (only differing from other people in his harmless habit of coming through doors without opening them), remembering how bewildered I'd been when I discovered that nobody else could see him. I'd known him for years, and we'd always been on the best of terms till, shortly before my illness, my mother had told me I was getting too old for such fancies. Though she'd spoken kindly, after this I was no longer at ease in my mind about him and wished he would stop coming to see me – but it was impossible to say this to an old friend – as henceforth his visits would have to be kept secret. Later, while I was lying in bed (though I knew I couldn't be scolded for anything till I was well again), the problem her words had raised weighed so heavily on my sick brain that I used to implore him to go away when he stood looking down at me reproachfully, and afterwards beg her to tell me he hadn't really been in the room.

Now, in the same way, I longed to call out, 'None of that really happened, did it?' But she, as if suddenly tired, had sat down at the scrubbed table, on which she rested her arm, deliberately placing her head upon it as if she'd just decided to take a nap there. Only she never took naps in the daytime; and I knew that, if by some chance she were to do so, it would certainly not be with her head on the kitchen table.

So the nightmare was still going on, though I could stand no more of it. And when I realized that she was quietly crying this was the last straw. Absolutely at the end of my tether, I lifted up my voice and started to weep aloud, making a lugubrious duet of our mutual grief.

I don't remember any more of that day's events. Curiously, I wasn't troubled again, at least not consciously, by feeling responsible for my father's mad actions, and if there were consequences below the surface I failed to recognize them.

My mother never talked to me about his pacifism, keeping from me all the unpleasant publicity the case attracted. I've no doubt she meant to shield me from her own unhappiness by saying nothing, but it might have been better for me if she'd been less restrained, for I couldn't help being aware of the conflict between them, which changed the whole atmosphere in which we lived. I see now how close to each other they must always have been, so that they were too absorbed in their personal tragedy to consider how lost and bewildered I felt, deprived suddenly of my importance as a part of the family unit – one that was breaking up – both of them too preoccupied to think much about me. But at the time I could not understand their apparent indifference to my feelings. Though there were no arguments in my presence, I'm sure my mother did everything in her power to dissuade my father from his new opinions, making use of every weapon at her command – blandishments, as well as appeals and denunciations. It must have been hard to convince her that he couldn't be shaken, but, once she was convinced, the thing obsessed her, and she persuaded herself that he'd disgraced us all. Since her nature was too gentle for bitterness, she lapsed then into a state of aggrieved melancholy, withdrawing into herself more and more, seeing no one, staying indoors and doing all the housework, dismissing the maid we had employed for years. When my father protested that it was too much for her and that there had been no need to get rid of the girl, she replied in terms of veiled reproach, somehow implying, so that even I half understood, that his principles were to blame, as though he'd deliberately imposed on her this penance of drudgery and isolation.

I was too young to understand what a great trial it must have been for the poor man, who was certainly still devoted to her, or to appreciate the rather touching humility with which he deferred to her in all things apart from his own views, as if trying to compensate for the one unforgivable deviation by waiving his right to assert himself in any other way whatsoever under his own roof. Naturally, I felt hurt because he didn't concern himself with my upbringing, seeming to take no interest in the, to me, all-important question of my going to school. This had been arranged for the autumn, but was now indefinitely postponed – officially on the grounds that it would be good for me to run wild for a bit after my illness, though I gathered that in some mysterious way his pacifism was responsible for this, too.

Looking back, I think he must have given his word not

to influence me towards his beliefs and scrupulously inter-preted this promise as meaning he must have no contact with me at all, since they were so important a part of him as to appear in every action and word. But, as nothing was explained to me at the time, I could hardly fail to resent the fact that he never asked me to be his companion at home or on his long solitary walks, but seemed, indeed, to avoid me altogether.

Inevitably, I blamed him for the changes that had come about since his return in my mother, to whom I no longer felt close as I'd always done before, and in my surroundings. In these few weeks the whole atmosphere of my home had changed and become sad, silent, secret. My father himself spent most of his time in the little room he used as a study, working for the various organizations which were trying to preserve the precarious peace of that time, whose represen-tatives occasionally came to see him. I can't imagine my gentle mother refusing to let these people in, so I suppose it was out of consideration for her that he always admitted them personally and later saw them off the premises, thus, in my eyes, investing their comings and goings with a con-spiratorial quality that contributed to the general secretive-ness.

It goes without saying that I didn't actually *think* in this way. Only, at odd times, while I was in the garden, perhaps, lost in fantasy or playing one of my involved ritual games, *the feeling* would fall on me like a stone, temporarily crush-ing imagination and interest – the feeling of the closed box that was my home, to which, ultimately, I must return, in which my parents were shut away from each other and from the world, each in silence and separateness, alone.

The cottage even began to *look* secret to me, the half-drawn shades at the upper windows suggesting the oblique glances of partially veiled eyes. And the rooms, now that they saw no more social life, developed a queer private life of their own. Often, when I opened a door, I would get the impression of wild activity just arrested, as though the different objects around me had only that moment dashed back to their usual places, where they were waiting impatiently for my departure, so that they could go on with their own affairs. I used to tell myself that one day I'd find out what they were up to by flinging open the door so suddenly that they'd be caught unawares. But I can't really have been very curious – or, more probably, I was scared of intruding – as I never did try to take them by surprise. Perhaps it was simply that I didn't have time, for it was summer, and I was always in a hurry to escape into the open air.

Before, my home had been a warm, happy place where I loved to be. But now I was always slightly uneasy indoors. It was a little frightening to think of my father being there all the time, so close, but invisible, unapproachable, like God. And my mother's silence made me uncomfortable, too. She spoke very little to me these days, and when I chattered as usual seemed not to hear, going about her perpetual cleaning with a shadowy withdrawn face, as if dedicated to cleanliness and to nothing else in the world. Though she always cared meticulously for my bodily needs, and even made an occasional effort to play with me, I couldn't help being aware that she had begun to live somewhere else and gave nothing of herself to anyone any more, not even to me. I soon got used to her endless washing and dusting and polishing, as I did to the tears that so often came into her eyes for no evident reason. I ceased to be affected by them, or so I thought, and would pretend not to notice that she was crying. All the same, I identified her continuous incomprehensible grief with all that confused and troubled me in my changed background, and when I thought of home now, I thought of her gliding soundlessly about her work in the shadows, like a dim tearful ghost.

Whenever I could, I tried to escape this dismal atmosphere by rushing out of doors; but *the feeling* would still be there, inescapable, ready to drop on me at any moment, crushing out any natural impulse of playfulness I might have had, so that I didn't know what to do with myself, didn't know how to get through the long hours. Because in the autumn I was neither to go back to the village school I'd been attending nor to a new school, and because nothing else had been settled about me, I felt utterly lost, stranded in a sort of limbo between my future and past.

I can still recall the queer, empty sensation of having run down like a clock that needs winding; a sensation with which I wandered about, listlessly, aimlessly, in the warm, humid, overcast weather, all the time vaguely expectant, always hoping for someone to take charge of me, wind me up and set me going again – though when this actually happened I was quite unprepared. How gladly I'd have welcomed my tall thin friend, who had clearly taken offence at being asked to go, for he never appeared, even though I made the round of our former meeting places each day.

In an attempt to anchor myself somewhere, I took to going to the paddock adjoining the school where we used to play in the afternoons. Now it was holiday time, but a few children lived there all the year round. Known to the rest of us as 'the orphans' – not contemptuously but in self-defence – these boarders formed a powerful union, secret society or exclusive club, from which others were for ever barred. By climbing the steep bank from the lane and crawling through the hedge I could lie in the tall weeds and grass on the other side without danger of being seen, enviously watching the orphans' noisy games, storing up the sound of their laughter and cheerful talk as a kind of insurance against the silence and solitude in which I passed my own days, dreaming that I was one of them, admitted to their lively, carefree companionship.

It would have been a very simple and natural thing, it seems now, for me to have revealed myself to my ex-schoolmates and turned the dream into reality. But it never occurred to me then. Nor was it because of the orphans' exclusiveness that the thought of approaching them didn't enter my head. At this impressionable age I'd already been so affected by the changed atmosphere in which I lived that the idea of playing with other children seemed quite unreal, something only possible in imagination – in fact, I half suspected the orphans of belonging to the same unmentionable category as the tall, thin man.

For this reason I concealed my trips to the paddock, preparing an alternative story as an alibi, in case my mother, in one of her unpredictable fits of noticing me, should ask, out of a sense of duty, what I'd been doing. I never dawdled in the vicinity either, though the chances of being seen and recognized were extremely slight – too slight to worry me, when, having crept through the hedge, I caught sight one day of the delicate, feathery fern-like leaves and pinkish stems of a certain plant the village people called the 'headache plant', which always fascinated me on account of its name and the odd medicinal smell of its crushed leaves.

There was just room for me to balance between the hedge and the six-foot drop to the lane. By leaning over precariously, I managed to grasp a handful of the faintly hairy leaves, crushing them in the process, so that I only had to take up a more secure position before I inhaled, closing my eyes as I did so the better to appreciate the mysterious bitter scent. Perhaps I hadn't recovered entirely from the after-effects of my illness, for, as I remember that peculiar odour, it seemed to contain an indescribable heavy languor, some fever quality of these interminable sultry days, of summer drowsiness turned ominous by the unfulfilled threat of thunder.

To the observer, of whose approach I wasn't as yet aware, I must have looked a queer little image, perched up on the bank with my hands full of headache plant and my eyes shut tight. A slight sound made me open them hurriedly, and there, to my surprise, was a great black car bearing down upon me, rolling downhill almost silently, filling almost the whole width of the lane.

I knew the car at once, for it was often to be seen outside our front door. But it didn't occur to me to wave to the occupant or to make any sign of recognition – not because I was surly or shy, but simply because I'd got so accustomed to being alone and unnoticed that I felt rather as though I were invisible. I was quite unprepared for the great black beetle of a thing to stop just below me and for the driver to put his head out of the window and invite me to jump in. It was more a command than an invitation, I thought, having long ago classified him as one of the order-givers of the world, pre-destined to command the obedience of his fellow men.

He was an old friend of my father's, this Mr Spector – the only one, I heard later, to brave public opinion by openly declaring the fact at this time, in spite of his own dis-approval of pacifist ideals. He often said that what he called 'the 'ologies' had nothing to do with friendship, politics and philosophy and the rest belonging to the intellect, whereas friendship came, or should come, from the heart – one's heart always told one to stand by a friend, especially if he happened to be down on his luck, and that was all there was to it. When I was a little older and heard how my father had begged him not to endanger his career by coming to see us, and how he had replied by coming rather more often, I was filled with admiration for such selfless nobility. But, at the time of this meeting, all I knew of him was that he seldom took any notice of me, from which I assumed that he disliked children, and I kept out of his way, slightly intimidated by his dignified, stern appearance and authoritative manner.

I wondered now what he could possibly want of me, as I scrambled down, obediently but rather reluctantly, and squeezed my skinny frame into the car, automatically taking care not to open the door beyond the very few inches it was possible to open it without touching the bank. I don't know whether this consideration was the result of training or some inherited feeling for orderliness and respect for inanimate things. Anyhow, it was useful to me now, for I found out, years afterwards, that this door situation was the first of a long series of character tests devised by Mr Spector for gauging my tendencies and development, and that his real interest in me originated in my ability to pass it with flying colours at such a tender age.

However, if he looked at me approvingly, I didn't notice it. I was far from comfortable sitting beside him, being secretly worried about what would happen if we met another car coming the opposite way, as well as uneasily conscious that I was untidy and dirty, and that the scraps of leaves and twigs I'd collected upon my person showed an embarrassing tendency to transfer themselves to the upholstery. My awkward attempts to remove them resulting only in more dust being deposited there, I glanced apprehensively at my companion, who said kindly, 'Never mind that', smiling in a much friendlier way than I'd ever expected.

From that moment all my worries were over, for he began

talking to me so easily and naturally that we might have been equals and old acquaintances. I asked the question that was bothering me, and it was settled at once, and my mind set at rest, by his answer that the other fellow would just have to back to the nearest crossroads, which I took as quite right and proper, never doubting for one instant that every vehicle on the road would unquestioningly give way to this assured and dominant personage.

I don't remember what we talked about at first, only that he spoke to me without a trace of the condescension grown-ups so often displayed in their conversations or of the foolish facetiousness some appeared to consider suitable to my age. It seemed such a very long time since I'd had a friendly con-versation with anyone, or that anyone had taken an interest in me and my affairs, that I was only too glad to go on talking about anything and everything under the sun. Mr Spector listened, always with the same grave attention, as if we were discussing important matters that concerned him personally, putting in an occasional question to lead me on, so that I revealed, I dare say, much more of my loneliness and bewil-derment than I realized. He asked me what I'd been doing up on the bank, and I explained about the headache plant, a few wilted leaves of which I produced and held up for him to smell, so that he could get an idea of its mystic properties. From there it was an easy and natural step to the orphans and my imagined companionship with them and how much I wished it were real.

As I sat there, enjoying myself thoroughly now, my hair stirred by the breeze our speed evoked from the stagnant air, a warm feeling of gratitude spread through me towards the man at my side, who, simply by letting me talk, had afforded me the relief I most needed. His questions never embarrassed me, for he never pressed for an answer. Nor did he burden me with comments or advice unless I asked him directly, in which case he would reply in a simple straightforward manner quite acceptable to me. I noticed that at certain moments our talk seemed to approach something dangerous or painful for which I could find no words, and I got the impression he understood these things that troubled me, but of which I couldn't speak because it was impossible for me to explain them or fit them into the frame of the language I knew. He somehow contrived to convey to me, without actually mentioning it at all, that everything would be clear to me when I was older, and that there was nothing to worry about, which I found inexpressibly comforting. I was convinced that he understood me without the need for speech, for he always seemed aware of these obscure danger points, and before I'd had time to grow really uneasy he'd have steered the conversation to a safer topic. My confidence was won absolutely. I felt more contented than at any time since my father's return, because this stranger, so sure of himself and of everything, so admirable, as I thought, in every respect, considered me worthy of his friendship and took an interest in my small doings, thus giving my ego a much-needed lift.

We had driven a long way round to give me time to finish all I had to say and were returning now by a route unfamiliar to me. I was very sorry the drive was over, for I'd have liked it to last for ever, but Spector again made things easy for me by taking this particular road, the strangeness of which occupied my attention and diverted my thoughts. Like many roads in our district, it was sunk between high banks topped by hedges, which here had been allowed to grow up till they formed a roof overhead. On this dull day, it was like driving along a green tunnel, filled with a curious watery twilight, in which floating pools, threads and ripples of brighter light were continually trembling and shifting, so increasing the aquatic effect.

Half my mind was given up to pretending that we were travelling on the ocean floor, when, suddenly and most unexpectedly, a cottage appeared in the distant circle that was the tunnel's mouth, very minute and clear, as if seen through a giant's green telescope. It looked so strange and remote that I didn't recognize it at once as my home. It had to my eyes the unreal miniature air and the slightly sinister charm of a fairy-tale cottage in an enchanted wood, and even when we arrived I wasn't exactly happy about going inside.

Nothing ominous or fearful, however, could exist in the proximity of Mr Spector, who, as soon as we'd stopped, took my hand in a friendly grip, ostensibly to help me out of the car, but really, as I knew, to assure me that everything was as it should be at home.

The rest of his visit followed the usual pattern, except that at one point, when both my parents happened to be in another part of the room, he gave me a slow deliberate wink; it had an extremely droll effect in his rather solemn face, so that I nearly burst out laughing. But afterwards I was very glad he'd substantiated our friendship and understanding in this way, as otherwise I certainly wouldn't have dared to believe in it, it seemed so excessively improbable.

We all went to see him off when the time came, and I remember that, while saying goodbye to my father and mother, he put his hand for a moment on my shoulder and said to them over my head, 'This young man of yours looks a bit peaky to me, as if he could do with a good blow of sea air.' Then he climbed into the low-slung car and went beetling off. I watched the bright metal hub of each wheel turning faster and faster, till I could distinguish the individual turns no longer. He waved once and was gone.

During the next few days he was much in my thoughts; I hoped he would come and see us again soon and that he would take me out for another drive so that we could resume our talk. Then one evening my mother told me that the orphans were being taken to the seaside for a month and that I was to go with them, and after that I could think of nothing else.

I never found out whether Mr Spector actually arranged this himself or whether the hint he'd given my parents had been enough, but, in any case, he was responsible for one of the happiest holidays I've ever had.

So much happened to me during that month at the seaside, each day was so full of exciting and memorable events, that the individual days seemed a week long yet the month itself passed in a flash. The day of departure, at first so astronomically remote as to be unthinkable, suddenly took a great leap forward and was right upon us. It seemed to me I'd no sooner arrived and begun making friends with the orphans (who proved unexpectedly easy to know now that it wasn't term time), and with them becoming acquainted with the fascination of sands, cliffs, rocks, concert parties, shrimping, sailing, swimming and a hundred and one other attractions, than I was back again at the station, reluctantly boarding the train that was to take us away from all these wonders, clutching a long wet ribbon of seaweed, and grimly resisting all adult efforts, both forcible and persuasive, to take it away from me.

Then, finally, it was evening, I was home again, the remains of the seaweed, much the worse for wear, still wound around my wrist. And my mother's slight figure, like a shadow itself, was gliding to meet me out of the thick shadows in our little hall. I kissed her and rushed to hang up my precious trophy at once, waving the battered, dank strand I had persistently dragged in and out of trains and taxis, lavatories, waiting-rooms, dining-cars, till now, like regimental colours tattered in many campaigns, it came home at last to rest in the place of honour. 'It's a barometer, you know; you feel it, and if it feels wet it's going to rain.' Over the years, I can still hear my voice, shocking in that silence where no voices were ever raised, loud, triumphant, insistent with youth and with my new independence.

I'd hardly thought of my home all the time I had been away. And I remember how I glanced around me now with a sort of wonder, as the feeling of it came back, and I saw that everything was just the same as it had been before: the hushed heavy silence and the shadows that seemed more real than the figures which they surrounded. Only *I* wasn't the same; I was tremendously, splendidly different. I'd come back as a conqueror, confident in myself and my health and vitality and in my ability to get on by myself in the real world among real people. Nevertheless I was struck by something implacably hostile in this remembered atmosphere, as the stubborn intractability of things and circumstances made itself felt, opposing my childish will. But I refused to be influenced by it; I was the victor returning triumphant, and would not be discouraged or silenced. Loudly I went on recounting my adventures and exploits and all that I had been doing.

Though not boisterous nor boastful by nature, I must have seemed so on this occasion, so determined was I to assert myself against this vague *something* in the air I felt to be inimical to me. My shadowy mother seemed to become more wraith-like under the bombardment of my ceaseless voice and relentless activity, as I rushed from room to room, opening and shutting doors, upstairs, downstairs, bringing out of my suitcase treasures I'd collected, all in a flood of talk, reminiscences, as if by myself alone I could fill the cottage with all the noise and liveliness the orphans would have made together, and so beat the silence and the shadows on their own ground.

The only room I didn't go into was my father's study, which I avoided purely from instinct and force of habit, without a thought for its occupant. It was only when I was completely breathless, and my spring of words had temporarily dried up, that it even occurred to me to ask how he was. For the first time I really looked at my mother, seeing the collection of miscellaneous garments draped over her arm. Because my own association with packing was so fresh in my mind, I knew at once what she had been doing when interrupted by my arrival, even before she said, 'You've come back just in time to say goodbye to your father. He's going away tomorrow – abroad.'

Her words dispersed a nameless apprehension that the thought of packing aroused; this was news I was not only relieved but delighted to hear. Remembering how happy I'd been while the two of us were alone, I imagined that history would repeat itself and I be restored to the importance I'd then enjoyed as sole object of her interest and affection. And, my expansive warmth overflowing, I was ready to love my father because he was leaving us in the morning. But the next moment I was almost hating him for the same reason, sensing that my mother was more preoccupied than usual on his account. This was *my* hour. *I* was the returning hero. He had no right to steal my place as the central figure. 'Where's he going? Why? Is it a long way off?' I insistently asked, not interested, just trying to fix her attention, for I saw that her thoughts had already left me.

All of a sudden she seemed to reach a decision in her own mind, replying most unexpectedly, 'You'd better ask him yourself.' I stared incredulously, as hitherto all contact between us had been discouraged. 'Yes, go and talk to him now while I get the supper – tell him I sent you.' She spoke with a decisiveness she hadn't displayed for a very long time. Then, smiling, went out of the room.

Knowing she wouldn't want me in the kitchen, I was left in perplexity, faced with the alternatives of my father's company and that of the silence and shadows. The silence became obtrusive now that I was alone; it seemed to be rising around me in a slow tide, steadily submerging all my bustle and noise. A clock began to strike in another room. I listened, counting the strokes, and when they were over the silence seemed deeper, more formidable. Old associations were starting to undermine my self-confidence, so I hastily reminded myself that I'd been away from home on my own and managed quite well. I was now independent; I wasn't afraid of anything or anyone, I informed the study door as I opened it, and said aloud, 'Mother sent me and told me to tell you so.'

I'd so seldom been in this room that I glanced around it now with a slightly nervous curiosity, half relieved, half dis-appointed to note its already partly dismantled air – books gone from the shelves, the pigeonholes of the desk empty, torn paper piled in the grate – more pathetic than gruesome and quite devoid of the sinister secrets I'd been expecting. My father, too, was almost disappointingly unalarming, a quiet, grave, unassuming man, looking up at me in surprise from the open case in which he was packing the last of his papers.

If, unbeknown to me, any ogrish dustbin-stamping image still haunted the dark recesses of my memory, it should have been exorcized now, as, in one of those odd isolated flashes of detached observation that children sometimes have, I saw how much older and wearier he was looking than when he'd come home to us from the war, far more worn and depleted by his fearful interior war of principles versus affection, of which I, of course, could know nothing. His ideals now triumphant, he was abandoning all he loved; the terrible battle was won. But he didn't look like a man who had won any sort of a battle; he only looked tired and lonely – very tired, and very lonely.

These were the impressions I recorded, camera-like, on the spot without understanding, and stored away to be re-examined at a much later date, when I was of an age to grasp their implications. At the time, I was only a resentful child, understanding nothing, absorbed in my own affairs, seeing him as the thief who had stolen first my mother and the happiness of my home and now my big moment.

When he came to me and took my hand, I, determined to make no concessions, stiffened against him without a word. He stooped to peer into my face, trying to see what was wrong, wondering, no doubt, why I stood there so woodenly, stubbornly silent. Then, puzzled, but asking no questions, he led me to the desk, where he sat down, producing some brightly coloured travel folders and began to tell me about his voyage and the countries he was going to visit, in such a gentle, friendly, quiet way that I melted slightly in spite of myself and asked why he was going away when he hadn't been back with us long.

He told me he was going to look for a country where there was peace, where people lived together in friendliness and goodwill, and the air wasn't poisoned, as it was here, by hatred and the bitterness of old wars or the fear of new ones. Somewhere on earth there must be a place where people were still sane and healthy and loved life, not death, and he was going to find it. Then he'd come back for us, and we'd all live there happily ever after.

He didn't, of course, use those exact words; I can't reproduce his language. I only know it all had the sound of a fairy-tale to me, so that I never thought of it as a reality, as a thing that really might happen. It didn't sound like a real project, and I remember thinking this promised land of his was just a device he employed (as I used my imaginary worlds) to escape the pains and disappointments of real life. It gave me a fellow feeling with him to know we shared these insubstantial resources, but it also seemed pitiable, almost shameful, that a grown-up person should be forced to descend to such strategems. When he said something unintelligible to me about peace being his home, I got impatient, reminding him that our country was at peace now, so there was no need for him to search for it in far-off foreign places. But this he wouldn't admit, shaking his head, saying, 'No, not real peace; and not for long, even such as it is. There won't be any more real peace – not here – not in our time.'

My interruption may have recalled him to the need for making himself comprehensible to a small boy, for he talked no more about peace and went on to tell me I'd have to be the man of the house while he was away and take care of my mother but that if anything went wrong I could always call upon Mr Spector, who had promised to run down occasion- ally to keep an eye on us both.

Mr Spector had almost disappeared from my memory, eclipsed by newer faces and by all that had been happening to me since I saw him, so I really don't know why I should have expressed such pleasure at the prospect of having him as a sort of father-substitute, unless, as I've sometimes thought, children have an instinctive knack of tormenting their elders without knowing how or why, and I was trying to let my poor father see how unfavourably he compared with his friend. I wasn't entirely innocent or ignorant of the hurting effect of my attitude, for I remember feeling slightly confused and turning aside to hide my embarrassment by inspecting the travel pictures, in one of which a boy of about my size was shown surf-riding, which interested me extremely, because I'd seen surf-riding, though of a very inferior kind, on my holiday. This was the real thing, I thought, gazing in awe at the huge breakers, imagining that I was that small figure, riding so splendidly on the backs of the surging swells, feeling the double thrill of speed and of dominion over their power. When my father asked if I'd like to go there with him and learn how to ride the waves, the word 'Yes' was actually on my lips when I suddenly checked it. Suddenly I was ashamed of being won over so easily, as if I'd foolishly let him trick me out of my resentment, like a baby bribed with a sweet, and I said 'No' almost roughly, pushing the picture away with an aggressive movement so that it fell on the floor.

He looked at me in astonishment, but he didn't reproach me or ask why I'd behaved so rudely. I heard him give a deep sigh; that was all. Then he stooped and picked up the folder I'd dropped and sat twisting it absently between his knees, his head bent, in a dejected resigned posture, as if my hostility were only what he'd expected and deserved. He said nothing more but, by making no further attempt to establish friendly relations, seemed to accept our estrangement as permanent. I felt he regarded the position as hopeless, and it rather alarmed me that this should be his final evaluation. Things seemed to have gone too far, further than I'd intended. I think I must now have seen how my behaviour had hurt him, accentuating his loneliness (of which I recall an impression almost concrete, as if he sat there under a glass dome), for I suddenly wanted to explain that I hadn't meant what I'd said but would really like very much to go with him and learn how to ride the waves. But, with the transparent wall between us, I couldn't reach him. Besides, I was becoming slightly unnerved by the long silence, and I couldn't take responsibility for breaking it.

I've often wished since that I'd been even a few years older at this time, so that we could have understood one another, at least partly, and I could have given him some of the companionship he so badly needed. He must have been desperately lonely and miserable, alone with his heart-breaking interior struggle, loving my mother so much and seeing her so unhappy. I like to think that, on this last evening, she relented a little and that they came nearer together again – though then, in my child's egotism, I resented even such tentative signs as they gave of a revival in understanding.

All this time, my father had kept the same crushed and despondent pose; now he suddenly sat up straight, his whole aspect changed, and gazed past me with an eager expectant look, as if a welcome visitor were appearing. So striking was the change in him that I looked around to see who was coming. There was nobody at the door, and though it opened a moment later only my mother came in to call us to supper.

He was already beside her before she had finished speaking, having crossed the little room with two or three rapid strides; and I heard him say, 'That was generous of you', while he stared into her face as if memorizing each feature.

'Oh, well . . . it's your last chance . . .' Her words hung in the air, with a sense of incompleteness, as if she'd have liked to say something more but was unsure of herself or else didn't know what to say. I was amazed, being used only to hearing her speak to him shortly and indifferently or in tones of self-pity or disapproval. She didn't move away at once either, as I expected, but for a few seconds returned his gaze; and though she was often uncertain and hesitant, this present hesitancy seemed different and more like shyness, almost like a young girl's. I, of course, had no notion what their remarks meant (years passed before it dawned on me that he wouldn't, even that night, have spoken to me without her permission), and the caprices of their adult behaviour were without interest to me. I was only concerned because I seemed to be losing my audience altogether. Determined to recapture and hold my mother's attention at any rate, I rushed across to her and, loudly exclaiming that I was starving, seized her hand and dragged her off forcibly to the dining-room.

The three of us sat down at the table. I had no feeling about it being the last time we would eat together, entirely taken up with my own importance, my own return and the adventures that had preceded it, which I was determined to relate in full. Nor had I any cause to complain of interruptions or lack of attention, for both my parents were singularly silent, allowing me to chatter away to my heart's content. Thanks to their quiescence and my exhilaration, this, my father's last meal under our roof, was probably the most normal, to outward appearances anyhow, of all those we'd shared since his return. We might have been any family group, consisting of over-indulgent parents and spoiled only child monopolizing the conversation.

I was very proud of myself that evening, extremely vain. But the day had been long and tiring for me, with the early start and all the excitement of the long journey and my homecoming, and now I was sitting up long after my usual bedtime. Suddenly, in the middle of a sentence, I was over-come by a tremendous desire to yawn, and, though I stifled it, another yawn soon followed, and this one was irresistible and could by no means be suppressed. I began to lose the thread of what I was saying, my tongue grew clumsy and stumbled over the words. Then my table napkin slid off my knees, and, diving after it, in the instant of semi-darkness under the table, I felt my eyes start to close, and I could no longer hide from myself the fact that I was terribly sleepy.

When I sat up again, the retrieved napkin dangling from one hand, everything seemed out of focus; the light pulsated with irregular beams, and every object conspired to elude and frustrate me. I thought I saw my parents exchange amused glances – a sign of friendly understanding so unprecedented that even then it caught my hazy attention. But I forgot to ask what the joke was, obliged to concentrate on the mechanics of eating. Though we were having some sweet I especially liked, I found an inexplicable difficulty in conveying it from the plate to my mouth. No sooner had I successfully captured a spoonful, the spoon immediately took flight and clattered down on the table some distance from me. I glanced at my mother to see whether she realized that it was the spoon not my clumsiness that was to blame, and suddenly I heard the strange sound, which I could hardly remember hearing, of my father's laughter, followed by the words, 'Take him off to bed quickly, for heaven's sake, before he falls in his plate!'

Too sleepy to resent this affront to my dignity, I was led from the room. I remember that, as I went, I kept stumbling and looking back, out of the owlish gravity of my near-dream, at the likeable smiling face that had mysteriously replaced my father's gravely remote one and wondering whether it belonged to the dream shapes around me.

I've a dim recollection of staggering drunkenly up the

stairs, sagging against my mother's supporting arm as she heaved and dragged me along like a sack of potatoes, and then of standing passively in my little room, swaying and dead with sleep, while she undressed me, pulling off one garment after another, and finally tucked me up in bed as she'd done when I was a baby. I came awake just sufficiently then for a muddled memory of two different fathers and of my own unkind words, which I must unsay in case the nice brown smiling face were the real one. Dimly, after that, I remained aware of my mother collecting my scattered clothes but was sound asleep before she left the room.

I slept late the next morning and came down to find the hall full of luggage and my father at the telephone engaged in a cryptic one-sided conversation of which I heard not a word, as I stood staring at him, endeavouring to decide whether he could be the agreeable person of whom I'd caught sight the previous night. Anyhow, I could afford to be generous since he was going away; I would give him the benefit of the doubt and tell him I should have said 'Yes', not 'No', to his question about surf-riding. This I decided as my mother, in a disciplinary mood I'd almost forgotten (I welcomed it as an indication of how quickly things would go back to what they had been as soon as we two were alone again), took me off to the dining-room, sat me down, put my breakfast before me and left me to eat it alone in front of the window.

This window was the only one facing north, with a view of the road, winding across rough meadows, past our door and on to still more remote dwellings among the woodlands and hills, which was our one line of communication with the rest of the world. Glancing out with my mouth full, I saw a car in the distance and realized that it must be the taxi coming to fetch my father. I hadn't known he was leaving so soon, and my impulse was to rush to him immediately while there was still time to talk; for, during the last few moments, the idea of an explanation had established itself as an urgent necessity, as though, in the mysterious secret life that went on concurrently with my normal existence, I'd just found out that some disaster would happen if he were to go away thinking me rude and unkind.

I was actually half out of my seat when my muscles suddenly relaxed, I subsided again and sat still or, rather, spellbound, reality sinking into abeyance, as I crossed the frontier of my magic world (as in those days I quite often did) without noticeable transition.

The shapes of everyday life still in front of my eyes, I sat motionless, staring out of the open window, watching the car pass a group of cattle, which plunged into brief awkward flight, tails rigid and udders swinging. Nothing in the quiet cottage suggested that anyone but myself had observed the taxi's approach. I was the only person, so far, who had seen it, which, in terms of magic, gave me absolute power over it. I could make it turn back, disappear – thus preventing my father's departure – simply by giving the sign. What *this* was I no longer remember – if, indeed, I ever knew. But I'm perfectly certain I really believed in my own power. It made me feel rapturous and triumphant. But there was also some horror in it; even as I exulted, I felt responsibility heavy on me as a concrete weight. It was as though I'd caught sight of some fearful doom, which I alone of all the inhabitants of the globe had perceived and could avert.

I knew I ought to give the sign that would alter my father's fate. But I didn't want him to stay at home; on the contrary, I was rejoicing because he was about to leave me alone with my mother once more. As I saw where my magic power would lead if I exercised it, all trace of exultance left me. Frightened and stupefied, I seemed to exist for a timeless moment in pure suspense, watching a race between his destiny and the car, relentlessly drawing nearer. Would I interfere before the taxi arrived, or let things take their course?

Just when the tension was becoming intolerable, it relaxed, releasing me from my entranced condition. Normality was restored, the material world re-established. All at once the flow of my natural everyday life continued. I was free to resume my usual activities and, jumping up, rushed out of the room, shouting, 'Here comes the taxi!' By running about and making a great deal of noise, I endeavoured to drown a lingering sense of havoc and fatality for which I was accountable on the other plane, in which attempt I was helped by the general bustling confusion.

The car had stopped outside the front door. Now the driver came in, joining my parents and the neighbour who was to stay with me, for I'd been told there wouldn't be room for all three of us and the luggage – a ridiculous error, about which I loudly and persistently protested, though nobody listened to me. In the turmoil created by four adults and myself, all picking up suitcases and putting them down again, I was continually getting in someone's way and being pushed aside. Suddenly I remembered what I had to say to my father but couldn't catch his attention till he went out to help the driver tie the heavier pieces on to the roof-rack, at which point I ran after him and started a breathless, incoherent speech, which he could hardly have been expected to understand. In any case, he was now called away, and I stood watching the driver knotting the rope as securely as for a journey to Samarkand. Wondering how the porter would ever unfasten it in time to catch the train, I forgot how my own time was running out and, with a shock, saw my mother dressed and ready to leave.

Before I could reach her, she had stepped into the car, and I could only prevent my father from following by throwing both arms around him and hanging on like grim death. In his usual gentle way, he bent down to ask me to release him. And, while he was doing so, my mother doubtless made a sign I failed to see to the plump countrywoman, who had retired a little way into the background to let us say our goodbyes in private, for I felt myself attacked from the rear. Knowing I wouldn't long be able to resist the strong arms that were pulling me back, I again began whispering urgent words, which probably made no sense at all to the harassed man. With a worried, perplexed look, he tried to follow what I was saying, in spite of the noise of the car, which had just started up, the scolding or loving cries of the woman tugging at me and my mother's repeated warnings that he would miss the train.

Considering all he had on his mind, it seems unlikely that he even remembered my childish rudeness, though it had wounded him at the time. But I felt it was profoundly important that he should understand me; I had a desperate sense of failure when, in response to increasingly agitated exhortations, he finally detached himself with some kindly phrase appropriate to my age, leaving me to the soft heart and strong arms of my captor, who, thinking I'd been overcome by grief, pressed me so tightly to her big bosom that I could hardly breathe and crooned consolingly over my head.

Luck was on my side, for, as the taxi moved off, it backfired so loudly that she was startled into relaxing her grip for a second. Twisting around, I managed to free myself, raced after it and, with a flying leap, landed on the running-board. The window was down, I leaned into the car, crying, 'I didn't mean it last night. I would like to come with you to the waves . . .' repeating, 'I would, I would!' with a wild vehemence that surprised me.

Even then I couldn't be certain my father had understood. As far as I remember, he said nothing but, concerned, I suppose, for my safety, tried to get hold of me but was prevented by the jolting of the car and by that fact that he had to lean right across my mother, who further impeded him in her efforts to catch the attention of the driver. Oblivious of what was happening behind him, he drove faster and faster over the bumpy road.

I felt a hand on my shoulder. But before it could get a firm grip, the taxi lurched around one of the many bends. The centrifugal force that sent me flying tore my clothing from my father's hand and made him stagger back, as I landed in the long grass at the roadside. The noise of the motor diminished, and I was aware for a second of a great stillness and of a great many things all happening at once. The woman at the cottage door gave a shrill scream and started running towards me; with a rasping squeal the taxi braked sharply to a halt, skidding in the white dust, three heads poking out of its windows like so many question marks; a colony of ants, disturbed by my descent among them, rushed madly in all directions through the forest of grass stems; while, unperturbed by it all, a bird's song continued, minutely distinct, in the great inverted bowl of the sky.

Then I picked myself up, none the worse, for the thick summer grass had saved me from anything but minor bruises – and I'd learned as all children do, especially in the country, to fall painlessly. The three heads were still turned in my direction; but now the woman came up, running her hands over me, confirming that I'd suffered no serious damage, whereupon my parents waved their hands, their heads were withdrawn and the car drove on again.

I thought their behaviour heartless – they might at least have made sure for themselves that I'd broken no bones – and a slight resentment replaced my former anxiety. The shock of the fall had, in any case, already banished an obsession belonging more to my private inward existence than to my life in the outer world, to which I now whole-heartedly returned, taking advantage of the situation to play on the feelings of my temporary companion, who, always indulgent, could now deny me nothing, so that the time passed very pleasantly till my mother's return.

She, too, appeared to be in an unusually generous mood. Almost as if she felt slightly guilty, she brought me several small presents and fussed over my trifling injuries in a most gratifying fashion. I remember making much capital out of a cut on my knee, which looked worse than it felt, though it left a scar which remains to the present day. For some time afterwards I put up with the inconvenience of a bandage and hobbled about the place as a wounded hero – much to my own admiration, if to nobody else's.

Did my father have a clue, I've wondered since, as to what all the fuss was about? I had no chance of finding out, as I never saw him again.

Now that my father had gone abroad for an indefinite period and I had my mother to myself again, I assumed that we would revert to the pleasant, placid, uneventful life we'd shared before his return. But, though outward conditions were the same as before, we ourselves had altered. Then, I'd been a small child, scarcely more than a baby; but my summer holiday away from home and without my parents had hurried on my development. I had now acquired new interests and some independence.

My mother had changed even more, and though she at first made great efforts to become her old self she had lost for ever the special quality of imaginative playfulness that had made her such a satisfactory companion for me during the earlier time, when an intimate private warmth had seemed to enclose us. For a while I pretended everything was as before, but slowly I was forced to notice that we hadn't really come together again; there was still a distance between us, a gap which refused to close but which was gradually widening. A certain coldness was growing up.

Looking back, I can see how different I must have seemed in my budding independence – though I always thought then that it was she who had changed – and how this must have disappointed her, for I think, now my father had gone, she counted a good deal on resuming her old relationship with me. I, too, must have seemed to be breaking away, following his example. My refusal to become a baby again must have come as the final discouraging blow, reviving that tendency to sadness and brooding which created coldness around her and repelled affection. Of course, I didn't understand this at the time. All I knew was that, though there was no actual break in our relations, in some mysterious way they deteriorated till no real intimacy was left between us. It was as though she hadn't the heart to cope with me as I grew older but gave up, deciding to let me go my own way, for she made no more efforts to enter into my thoughts or doings. And I, finding her often sad and so preoccupied that she scarcely seemed aware of my presence, instinctively and in self-defence tried to make myself more independent, so that we automatically drifted further and further apart.

In these circumstances, I was glad to start studying under the clergyman of our parish. The rectory being some distance away, I had my lunch there and only came home in the late afternoon after I'd finished work. This odd little wiry man, with a fluff of saintly white hair, was something of an eccentric, an authority on the Roman occupation of our district, of which many traces remained, some of them already excavated under his supervision. He taught me Latin with enthusiasm, so that I soon became very good for a boy of my age and could even converse with him in this language at lunchtime. In our other subjects he took no interest, frequently abandoning them in favour of inspecting the site of some ancient villa or encampment, where I would take a hand with the digging or search the undergrowth for a rare species of edible snail, said to be descended from those the Roman legionaries had imported.

I was grateful to the rector for not talking down to me and treating me like a grown-up person – which probably made me rather precocious but saved me from wasting several years in overprolonged adolescence, like most of my contemporaries. He also gave me the run of his library, and I am indebted to him for my love of reading – one of the few pleasures not likely to be taken away from one in this life – though probably I wouldn't have become such an ardent reader all at once if it hadn't been winter when I was forced to spend the long evenings indoors, or if my mother had been more companionable.

Seeing me bent over the turning pages for hours on end, she would emerge from her meditations to ask what I found so absorbing. I'd have gladly given a detailed account of each book in turn, but she wasn't really interested, and, asking only from ulterior motives, her attention soon wandered. I think she half knew I used the books to replace the affection she no longer gave me and that this somehow made her dislike them. In her determination to stop me reading she displayed more interest in me than she'd done for some time, so that I was almost glad to be scolded, thinking it meant a revival of our lost warmth. That winter happened to be particularly severe, and I couldn't help feeling there must be some connection between the desolate frozen landscape outside and the coldness growing indoors. But though I tried to build up an interior glow as I built up the fires, an occasional scolding was insufficient fuel. She soon returned to her melancholy moods, when she seemed to want only to be left alone, and I had to resort to my books.

Our old trustful affection had already been left so far behind that I didn't hesitate to deceive her by keeping them hidden, doing my reading in secret, in bed, by the light of a carefully shaded candle or, in the daytime, in a private retreat of my childhood, behind the blackish foliage of an old yew tree. This treehouse, built for me by my father years before, had, since I ceased to play there, fallen into decay and its very existence been almost forgotten, totally concealed as it was by dense growth, so that, wrapped in rugs and blankets, I could read here without fear of discovery while I was supposed to be skating or engaged in some other healthy sport – I'd been told it was 'unmanly' to be such a bookworm and that I ought to get out more in the open air.

But, as the days shortened and the weather grew worse, I could avail myself less and less of this refuge. Inevitably, my pernicious habit of reading in bed was discovered and led to a scene, my mother accusing me of ruining my health and eyesight and endangering our lives – sooner or later, I was bound to set the place on fire with my candle. I think she would have gone on to forbid me to read at all if Mr Spector, who happened to be there at the time, hadn't interceded for me and persuaded her to adopt a more moderate attitude.

He'd been visiting us regularly ever since my father left,

but as I was always at the rectory when he came, only returning when he would be on the point of departure, we'd done little so far but exchange greetings. Now, however, by openly siding with me he won my gratitude, and I admired his tactful handling of the whole affair, which actually left my mother in a better mood. He stayed late that day on purpose to talk to me, and I was flattered – almost dazzled, indeed – by his friendliness and understanding, so that much of my original feeling for him revived on the spot. Afterwards this interview seemed very important, marking an irrevocable step, and from then onwards our intimacy progressed rapidly.

He now made a point of coming to see us at weekends when I was at home and also of spending some time alone with me on each visit, realizing my need to let off steam and encouraging me to speak of whatever was on my mind. He thus acted as a sort of emotional safety valve, for I trusted him implicitly and told him everything without hesitation.

At this time I was mainly worried about not going to school. Being the only pupil of an eccentric rector wasn't at all the same thing and seemed to single me out and make me undesirably conspicuous, so that I was not only conscious of my isolation but slightly ashamed of it. Now, to my great relief, I could tell him all this, in the triumphant knowledge that no sense of inferiority or loneliness could survive the fact that he – this powerful, wonderful, magnificent personage – was my friend.

The understanding between us even enabled me to speak of my mother. On one occasion I remember saying that, as she was unhappy herself, she didn't want anyone else to be happy and stopped me reading because she knew it was what gave me most pleasure. And I remember, too, how oddly he looked at me then. It has since occurred to me that it was a somewhat strange observation in view of my age and an instance of the precociousness I have mentioned. Possibly he looked upon it as a sign of intelligence and therefore increased his interest in me; but this is only a guess, for he merely nodded wisely, saying that there was something in my remark but that I must always be patient and gentle with her, and with all women, as they didn't have our resources. The last words, of course, puffed me up with pride, and I nodded back, sagely complacent, linking myself with him in a closed circle of superior masculine wisdom.

What I most appreciated about him was the impression he always gave of understanding everything and having everything under control, so that nothing disturbing could happen while he was there. He shared with his great black car the reassuring quality of infinite reliability, always arriving at the time arranged, no matter how bad the weather conditions, so that I began to believe them both immune from the tiresome impediments so frustrating to ordinary people.

Though he never took me out alone, I enjoyed driving with him more than anything else, particularly at this time of the year. There was a special thrill about being carried along by the powerful machine, so warm in this bitter weather that it really might have been an extension of its owner's self and warmed with his blood. To be borne with such speed, warmth and comfort across the bleak icebound landscape gave me a godlike feeling of superiority to the everyday world, which was the basis of countless fantasies, taking their changing form from the ever-moving vista before my eyes. I didn't resent my mother's occupation of the front seat but actually preferred this arrangement, where I could remain alone at the back without fear of being interrupted in my daydream. I would become so lost in my imaginings that I was completely oblivious of my companions' conversation, and even of their existence, sometimes brought back to earth with a start to find them laughing at my 'wool-gathering' and repeating some question or remark already made several times.

At the start, it rather surprised me that my mother, who had so little to say to me, always seemed cheerful and talkative on these outings. But I soon realized it was only another manifestation of Mr Spector's singular powers of controlling and directing all situations according to his will and prohibiting all that might be embarrassing or alarming. So convinced was I that his presence formed a guarantee against unpleasantness that it was a considerable shock to find this wasn't invariably the case.

The Sunday I'm thinking of was one of the coldest days in the whole winter. I was very keen on skating just then, but I rather envied the pair, whom I'd left sitting comfortably by the fire when I set off for the ponds. A biting northeast wind soon drove me off the ice, and I returned to find the cottage so silent that I assumed it was deserted and that they must have changed their minds about going out. As I dutifully took off my snow-caked boots in the porch, I told myself they wouldn't stay out long on such a day, feeling slightly peeved because they'd gone without me. Suddenly, then, I remembered a book I'd left by the fire and, to avoid restarting old arguments, hurried to fetch it, just as I was, in my stockinged feet, before they returned.

Convinced of being alone in the house, I was quite startled, on opening the door, to see the two of them still sitting there, though not precisely as I had left them, for my mother had abandoned her favourite seat to share the visitor's sofa – or so I thought, for I hardly had time to see anything before she sprang up, pushing the hair back from her face with a distraught gesture, and, in a voice trembling with anger or some other emotion, accused me of creeping about the house and spying on her. I was still blocking the door, too astounded to move, when she rushed up and thrust me aside and then fled from the room.

Speechless in my hurt amazement, I turned to Mr Spector, who hadn't stirred, quite unmoved, it appeared, by her extraordinary conduct. He might have been half asleep, lounging there in a relaxed pose, absolutely detached and calm. I was beyond reach of further surprise; but if anything could have astonished me more it was to hear him say dreamily, 'You've got a very beautiful mother, Mark', as though nothing else had struck him about her now. Yet I, too, in the midst of my confused feelings, had been not unaware of her usually pale cheeks flushed pink by anger or the heat of the fire and making her look extremely pretty – not that I saw any need to comment on it.

While I stood there, hopelessly at a loss, the man now signed to me amicably to sit beside him, which I did more or less in a daze. He slid his arm around my shoulders and drew me into a comfortable position, leaning against him, implying that nothing untoward could have occurred while we were sitting so pleasantly side by side.

'There's nothing to get upset about. She didn't mean it,' he said kindly, adding, 'I'm going to talk to you now as if you were grown-up.' After this flattering start, he went on to tell me that, in a few years' time, I'd find out for myself that all women were liable to caprices and nerve storms at certain times, irrational moments, when it was useless to reason with them, and they just had to be humoured, being, far more than men, at the mercy of the delicate mechanism of their bodies, which had the supreme gift of bestowing life.

I was already recovering, for his total composure made nonsense of the idea that anything disturbing could have happened. The fire's heat was almost stupefying after the icy cold out of doors. Staring into its glowing heart, I began to feel drowsy, as though this were all a dream, and when he next spoke his voice seemed to come from somewhere a long way off, far above me. 'You're a country boy, and you don't go about with your eyes shut; you've got a good idea, I expect, of the way nature works. But your father wanted me to have a talk with you at the right time, and this seems as good a time as any.'

He had a real gift, Mr Spector, of explaining difficult or obscure matters in terms suited to his audience, and I'm sure any parent or schoolmaster would have admired his presentation of the facts of life for my benefit, getting them forth without prudery or sentiment but simply and with delicacy of feeling. At first I listened sleepily, only half attending, but by degrees my interest was engaged, as it was bound to be by so absorbing a subject. He could have chosen no better way of diverting my thoughts from my mother's extraordinary attack. And when she came back after being out of the room a long time, we were talking as if nothing out of the usual had happened.

Whether she took her cue from us or had already decided to ignore the incident, I don't know, but anyhow she, too, acted as if everything were perfectly normal for the rest of the visit. Nor did she refer to her accusation when the two of us were alone, either that evening or at any time subsequently.

In a way her silence was a relief, yet in another way I resented it, as indicating my unimportance to her, not even worth an explanation of such hurtful, insulting words. I was more aware after this of the coldness, and the gap between us seemed wider.

We were both on edge during the next few days, and once, when she called me Marko (she still occasionally, to my annoyance, used this babyish name, originally given to tell me apart from my father, whose name was Mark, too), I lost my temper completely, said it sounded as if she were calling a dog and that I refused to answer to it any more. Why should I, after all, when there was no longer anyone to distinguish me from?

I can still see the little nervous jerky movement she made only when she was upset, glancing over her shoulder, as if some imp might have heard, exclaiming, 'How can you speak like that? Do you want to bring your father bad luck?'

Though I knew it was rude and heartless, I only laughed. Surely she wasn't so superstitious? She said no more, but, giving me a reproachful look, went out of the room – though not before I'd caught the glint of tears in her eyes.

I felt mean and ashamed. But I also felt she had taken an unfair advantage of me. Why couldn't she have got angry instead of crying, so that I could have answered back?

My thoughts kept reverting to her unwithdrawn accusation, and the unmistakably genuine agitation she'd shown while making it, which for some reason I could not fathom, disturbed me almost as much. Nor could I understand why my mind, as if of its own accord, had arrived at the conclusion that Mr Spector was much more closely connected with the incident than his judicial calm would have had me believe. In fact, the whole thing was a complete puzzle to me and a weight on my spirit.

No doubt I'd have forgotten it in due course. But before there was time for this, after an interval much shorter than usual, he reappeared. For the first time I felt slightly uncomfortable before him and was glad that he took my mother off at once to talk business, while I, the day being windless and sunny, though still very cold, announced that I'd go for a walk and retired to the privacy of the treehouse.

The word 'business' had for me lifelong associations with dullness and exclusively adult mysteries I neither wished, nor was expected, to understand, so that I felt excused from further attention and could relax with my unreal characters and their adventures, unperplexed by problems of grown-up behaviour. I became so absorbed in what I was reading that I didn't notice the two familiar figures emerge from the cottage till it was too late to think of escape. Now I was in an awkward dilemma, unable to declare my presence without declaring myself a liar and giving away my secret refuge as well. I could only keep quiet and try to escape the guilt of eavesdropping by making myself deaf to the conversation below, becoming so immersed in my book that I ceased to be aware of the speakers, as I did in the car.

All the same, I disliked extremely the idea of deceiving Mr Spector, particularly as, with the superstition I'd ridiculed in my mother, I was half afraid he would *not* be deceived but would somehow detect my presence, though I knew I couldn't be seen from below. I tried unsuccessfully to persuade myself that he'd excuse me in the circumstances, growing more and more nervous, as to become oblivious proved beyond me – there was no car noise to help me now, and the speakers, unaware of the need for caution, didn't lower their voices. In the quiet garden, my mother's emotional tones rang out so distinctly that I couldn't fail to hear every word.

'I might as well be a widow. I wish I were. At least I'd be free then, not in this impossible position, neither married nor unmarried but simply tied. Why should I have all the responsibility of marriage and nothing else while he goes about perfectly free? It's so unfair, leaving me here to bear it all alone. A boy needs a father; Mark's growing up without knowing his father at all. And what about me? I'm still young, but I won't be young for ever. Time keeps passing. Am I never to have a husband? Love? A real marriage?'

They had passed now and, their backs towards me, were walking away. But her complaining voice still hung on the hushed winter air, though I could no longer make out the words. Those I'd already heard, striking at the roots of all that was safe and settled in life, caused me a moment of childish panic. Their two figures had reached the shadow of the cottage crossing the sunlit grass like dark water. For a second I had the illusion of watching two strangers on the bank of a river, towards which the man seemed to be urging his reluctant companion, as if urging her to take the plunge. Growing more composed as they turned back to approach me again, I saw with my normal vision that my mother was calmer, Mr Spector doing most of the talking.

My heart gave a sudden jump at the sound of my name. Yes, it was my future he was now speaking about so earnestly, recommending that I should be sent to the school originally chosen for me, where an unexpected vacancy had come up at half-term. This was what I wanted more than anything, and my rather negative feelings for him swung to the other extreme: wonderful, kind, omnipotent Mr Spector, for whom the word 'impossible' didn't exist! I could hardly listen to my mother objecting that it wouldn't be fair to me or my father, that I'd be teased and bullied because of his views till I began to hate him. What rubbish! And why couldn't she see that if Mr Spector wished it to be so, so it would be? Never doubting that he was acting out of kindness and for my good, I identified myself with him completely, first impatient, then irritated, finally alarmed, by her persistent opposition. Suppose he took offence at her unusual obstinacy or simply got bored and abandoned the subject, abandoning me to my fate? He'd already carried on the argument on my behalf longer than could reasonably be expected of him.

But her opposition appeared only to make him more determined, to judge by the way he put his hand on her arm, forcing her to stop and, leaning slightly towards her, continued to speak in a low but vehement tone, bringing all his powers of dominance and persuasion to bear upon her. They were standing just below me; I could actually *feel* the intensity of his will fixed upon her. But instead of reassuring me it had the reverse effect. All at once I became uneasy and my excitement faltered.

Why should he be so eager for me to go to school? What did it matter to him? She murmured some further objection I didn't catch, which he at once overruled, keeping her all the time under his fixed and compulsive gaze. Such intensity seemed somehow excessive and disturbing, altogether too much to be displayed over my humble affairs. My uneasiness was now reinforced by a sense of mystification and doubt; something seemed to be going on under the surface of things which I didn't understand but which concerned me closely nevertheless.

They were already starting to walk away again, and I saw that she was about to give in, as I'd known she would do in the end. But now I suddenly found I'd changed sides. No longer under the man's spell, I felt uncertain and troubled. The thought that he wants to get rid of me, get me out of the way, flashed through my mind like lightning on a dark night, illuminating everything for a second, and then was gone.

Though I was too immature to grasp the idea, it had shaken my trust in him. I suddenly wanted to warn my mother, to let her know I was with her and against him. Was it some premonition of future events that made me want to run after her, seize her hand and hold her back from where she was going? Though I could have no adult understanding of her predicament, I must have felt an instinctive sympathy, for I remember thinking how frail and helpless she looked, how easily crushed, beside this large ruthless man, whom I saw as one with his great powerful car. What chance had she against him? Listening to the meaningless rise and fall of their receding voices, I tried vainly to think of some way of helping her. Poor star-crossed creature, lonely and discontented, she was denied even my childish support in the unequal contest between her defencelessness and the power of his worldly experience.

The sound of their voices ceased; they'd passed out of my field of vision. I waited a little, wondering if they would come back to this part of the garden, then, as I neither saw nor heard any more of them, realized they must have gone indoors.

Immediate restlessness overcame my disquiet. I could remain no longer in that restricted space. Cramped and chilled, I scrambled down to the ground, looking back once at the tree deliberately, with the thought that I'd probably made use of it as a hiding place for the last time. A new life, full of thrilling adventures and possibilities, lay before me. At last I was about to break out of the narrow compartment of childhood that had confined me so long. As if to leave it all behind me forthwith, I started walking away from the yew at a brisk pace, not noticing where I was going, absorbed in enthralling fantasies of the future.

My elation, however, quickly subsided, undermined by obscure forebodings. I couldn't help being aware of an inner discomfort growing stronger and more assertive at every step, till it occurred to me that I was really walking through the frozen fields to correct my untruthfulness on at least this one point. My conscience reminding me how I'd deceived Mr Spector, I at once turned back, deeply ashamed. How was I to face him? Should I pretend to know nothing about the conversation? But I knew I couldn't do that. My guilt would betray me; he'd certainly see through the pretence, if he didn't already know I'd been in the tree. The only thing was to be perfectly honest with him, but I had grave doubts of my ability to carry through this bold decision. I seemed to be more afraid of him than I'd realized.

The sun had gone down some minutes earlier, and the short winter day was ending when I arrived back at the cottage, where the big black car stood, monumental in the fading light. My childish imagination pictured some huge primeval beast crouching there, immobile but strangely watchful, a curious air of baleful alertness in the armoured snout and huge lamp-eyes swivelled slightly towards me. For a moment I wanted to turn and run, and though I continued to advance it was more and more reluctantly, keeping my eyes on the ground to avoid seeing the monster I identified with the man I'd deceived.

When next I looked up, darkness seemed appreciably nearer and so, of course, did the car. I had got quite close to it when, to my horror, the indistinct shape of the owner himself loomed up before me. Again seized by an impulse of flight, involuntarily, I turned away, then, disgusted by my cowardice, forced myself to confront him.

In the dusk, he looked to me larger and heavier, somehow menacing, indefinably changed, the same and yet not the same. I suppose my long acquaintance with the idea of magic gave me the notion that he must be two people at once, passing from one personality to the other as I moved between my two worlds. The idea itself alarmed me less than the obscure perception of characteristics not exactly benevolent in the second strange self, by which it seemed I might have been used for unimaginable ends. Yet my feeling for the man as a whole was unaffected or, if anything, heightened by the new factor of his dual being, which established, I felt, a more personal private bond between us. My greatest wish was to receive his forgiveness, and I immediately told him exactly what had occurred. I needn't have worried about not being brave enough to confess, for confession seemed my one hope. I completed the agitated account for my own sake, convinced now that I'd been right in suspecting he'd known about my deceit all along. I told him everything and became silent; there was no more I could do. I had thrown myself on his mercy and must await the verdict. If only he would forgive me and take me back into favour again! If he were to remain alienated from me I felt I couldn't bear it, as if our relationship meant more to me than anything in the world.

It can only have been for a very few seconds that he gazed at me after I'd finished speaking. But an eternity of silent twilight seemed to elapse, while I felt his unseen eyes delving into me with their strange penetrating intensity, exploring depths of the very existence of which in my childish being I wasn't aware, as though he were investigating me, not only as the child I was now but as the potential being liable to appear at subsequent stages of my development. But, when he finally spoke, he said only, 'I'm glad you told me; otherwise . . .' leaving the phrase incomplete, with a slightly menacing sound. Long afterwards, it struck me that the situation could have been one of his mysterious tests, and I wondered, if so, whether I'd failed completely or, to a limited extent, redeemed myself by confessing, as I was inclined to hope might have been the case.

He moved his hand then, I remember, and a small light

came on in the car among the dials and switches, casting a weird upward glow on his face, which, against the dusk, appeared larger than life, indestructible-looking and not quite human; a graven-image effect, lasting only an instant, before some slight change of attitude restored the Mr Spector I'd always known.

The formidable stranger had vanished without a trace, and, at the sight of my genial friend, unable to contain myself, I sprang towards him and grasped his hand, so over-joyed to feel his goodwill that I kept babbling promises, explanations, apologies, hardly knowing what I was saying, only delighted because I wasn't rebuffed. My overwhelming gratitude for forgiveness would, with the slightest encourage-ment, have led me into some fantastic extravagance – I'd have gone down on my knees before him or burst into tears kissing his hand – but, since I saw that any such demonstration would be unwelcome, these confused protestations were my only emotional outlet.

Though my thoughts were in a whirl, I knew I was speak-ing the absolute truth when I said that, whatever might happen in future, even if he were to change entirely one day, I would always, under all circumstances, remain loyal to him. What I envisaged by such a drastic change I don't know. But the fact was, I could do nothing else, for I felt bound to him by some tie stronger than love or blood. Suddenly I'd become conscious of his dual power over me and a little afraid of it, not altogether certain of its benevolence. But, though an element of fear and suspicion might henceforth be present in my feelings for him, it only seemed to increase my admiration, loyalty and attachment. At the same time, I recognized these feelings as being of a different quality from my former unthinking childish affection and trust, to which I knew I could never return.

Though my actual thoughts were much less lucid and precise, I was even then conscious of some new awareness, marking the end of my childish relationship to him. It didn't matter that everything was confused in my head, for I knew he would sort it all out for me. Now I had no secrets from him, and never could have, having submitted to a form of enslavement. It was an oddly relaxed and comfortable feeling, as though I'd opened myself like an untidy drawer and could sit back peacefully while he arranged the contents.

And he at once indicated his knowledge of the obscure processes going on in me by saying almost wistfully, 'Don't be in too great a hurry to grow up, Marko', using the diminutive of my name for the first and only time – strange that it should have sounded touching from him yet, when my mother used it, it only annoyed me. Recalling at this distance of time the regret in his voice, I sometimes wonder if one might presume to suspect that, for all his power, wealth and importance, he lacked something that could be found in the simplicity of a child's affection, but such speculations are unprofitable and lead nowhere. He said no more to me then but encircled me with his hard strong arm, and intimately entwined thus we went indoors together.

The rest of the evening, as I recollect it, was devoted to hurried arrangements, for it was decided that he should stay the night and drive me to school the next day, stopping at a largish town we passed through to buy me the necessary outfit.

Notwithstanding all the excitement, as soon as I was in bed I fell sound asleep. Yet, at some time in the night, I seemed to become aware of the familiar room, not quite dark, as if light from the passage were coming in through the open door, and of my mother standing beside me, a shadowy form, as I'd seen her on so many nights. I seem to think that, neither quite awake nor quite asleep, I reached up automatically as I used to do long ago and that she laid her head beside mine and whispered loving words, asking me to forgive her for not being a good mother and hoping I would be very happy at school. All the cold melted out of me in the warmth of her arms, and I felt we were just as close to each other as we'd ever been and that tomorrow everything would be different. It had all been a misunderstanding, a mistake.

But tomorrow was the day when I was going away, and, in the bright daylight, the night's shadowy happenings became so remote and vague that I couldn't be sure I hadn't dreamed them.

Looking back from the car, I suddenly seemed to see the cottage as it would be after we'd gone, and the thought of my mother left alone there made me feel guilty and sad. I remembered that my father had told me to take care of her, and my heart sank because I was abandoning her instead. There she stood at the door, waving, and already she was no larger than the painted lady who came out of the carved Swiss chalet when the summer weather was set fair. Next moment, both she and the cottage were out of sight. As the car rushed on, carrying me further and further away, I knew with curious certainty that I'd looked at her for the last time with the eyes of a child, that it was my childhood I was leaving behind me and that I'd never see anything in quite that same way again.

These thoughts are hard to describe. Not exactly melancholy, they produced rather a sense of pressure and transience. Once more I was going out into the world unsupported to fend for myself, as when I went for my holiday in the summer. But now, though there was some relationship still between us, I was no longer the child that had played with the orphans on the seashore. And, by the time I next saw my home, the relationship would have terminated completely; I should have changed into someone else, and the world would have changed, too, seen through those other eyes.

At intervals all through my life this sense of being *in transit* has overtaken me at odd times, though never more strongly than on this occasion when I was first conscious of it. Looking back dubiously at the child I had been and was leaving without having really known it or understood it, I wondered whether I'd always have to move on before getting to know myself properly.

It wasn't the time to discuss these things with my companion; there were too many distractions, and I gave myself up to them – as I've often regretted since – postponing serious talk to another occasion that never came. When we reached the town Mr Spector proceeded to provide me with a complete new wardrobe, more clothes than I'd ever owned before, and all of such superlative quality that I began to worry about the expense and lodged a timid objection. However, he only laughed and spoke of the importance of first impressions, going on to add various accessories not strictly essential and finally insisting on buying me new luggage to contain them all. Once I gave up trying to stop him and wondering how he would ever be paid back, I was very proud of my new elegant possessions. The thought of them gave me much-needed moral support when we arrived at our destination.

The grandeur of the school's medieval buildings intimidated me, and I was completely overawed by my first glimpse of the famous topiary chess-garden, of which I'd already heard. As the car slowed down, the grotesquely clipped fantastic tree shapes seemed to close in behind it, cutting off the familiar world, imprisoning us in their midst.

We stopped, and the dark heads bowed in mockery, the branches groaned, and I felt tentacles of antique malice already reaching towards me.

Staring at these grotesque evergreens, wide-eyed with wonder, I hardly noticed Mr Spector speaking to the porter, whose reply evidently failed to satisfy him, for now he suddenly strode towards the dim monastic-looking cloisters and intercepted one of the gowned figures passing to and fro there. He was only a junior master, I discovered later, but he looked very grand to me in his lined and hooded gown. I wasn't at all surprised at his indignation on being peremptorily requested to take us to the principal. What *did* surprise me, so that I forgot all about the malignant chessmen, was the way his whole manner changed, becoming almost obsequious, at the sight of Mr Spector's card. But I had no time to think or to sort out my impressions as we followed on his heels to the door of the Head's study, where a request to be allowed to prepare his chief was swept aside, as the man himself was, so that all three of us burst into the room together.

Though I didn't then fully appreciate the enormity of our conduct in thus invading this holy of holies, uninvited and even unannounced, I couldn't fail to see how angry the Headmaster was when he rose and, with an outraged expression, drew himself up to his full height, an imposing and menacing figure. But, to my astonishment, he, too, succumbed to the card's effect, just as his subordinate had done, surrendering unconditionally and even speaking a few stilted words of formal politeness – which, however, didn't spare him the indignity of hearing his own assistant dismissed by Mr Spector, who took his submission for granted.

'This is the boy I told you about,' he said, when the man

had hurriedly left the room. 'I want your assurance that his father is not mentioned, either to him or in his presence – it's the wish of his mother, who is rather oversensitive on the subject. Is that understood?' I listened amazed to this haughty voice of command, which must surely be the voice of that second, more formidable self, and scarcely noticed the affirmative answer; it seemed to me there could be no other. Yet it was the familiar friendly voice that now addressed me. 'Let me know at once if you have any sort of trouble – but I don't think you will.' A peculiar smile accompanied the last words, which seemed intended less for me than for the other man, to whom the speaker continued – quite incomprehensibly, as far as I was concerned – 'No censorship, mind. I'll be getting a full report myself, so any attempt at deception would be a mistake, wouldn't it?'

I was completely puzzled by this strange behaviour and the alternation of tones. Why was he treating the Headmaster so harshly? Even now, when the man had given in to him altogether, and his own manner appeared more genial, the geniality clearly covered a threat. But the moment I'd been privately dreading for some time had arrived, and, with unmistakable kindness, he said, 'I must be off. Write and tell me how you get on. And, remember, the beginnings of things are always apt to be difficult.' He spoke the last words in Latin, knowing I was familiar with the adage. Then, giving me an encouraging smile, hurried to the door, waving away the offer of an escort. 'No, I'll find my own way out.' The door closed behind him, and I was left to begin my new life alone.

The room suddenly seemed darker and gloomier, its narrow windows designed for the exclusion of enemies rather than the admission of light and air. An oppressive atmosphere reasserted itself, emanating, perhaps, from the shelves of huge, heavy books lining the walls. I was aware of these things, even while my mind framed consciously for the first time the question I've been asking myself intermittently ever since, 'Who is Mr Spector?' What sort of man could behave in such a high-handed manner and disperse the repressive power of centuries-old tradition, as he'd just done, letting a draught of cold air blow through these grim stagnant rooms, airless for so many years?

But I couldn't consider the question now, while the Headmaster was regarding me with a disfavour I quite understood, since I'd been the indirect cause of his humiliation. Looking at him as straightforwardly as possible, I could discern no pity in that hard, cold face; the face, as I was to learn, of a man who as an enemy was absolutely implacable. At this moment, I only saw that he'd been mortified and that someone must suffer for it and that I seemed the likeliest victim. I felt very small and helpless and lonely just then, cut off from all that was known to me, shut into a strange hostile world. The dark dismal room was as forbidding as if it belonged to a fortress – a prison. I had a momentary nostalgic vision of Mr Spector, driving away in his big car, leaving me further behind with every milestone.

But nothing happened to me, neither then nor later. Having surveyed me long enough to make me most uncomfortable, the Head turned away with a disgusted grimace, as though he couldn't stand the sight of me any longer. Matron would come and attend to me; I was to wait here for her, he coldly informed me, and then went out, letting the door close with a heavy thud, like the door of a cell.

I waited alone there for what seemed an age. At first, sounds came from other parts of the building. I heard distant shouts and closer voices of boys calling to one another;

mysterious bells rang, there was a stampede, a pounding of running feet. Then silence fell. I began to think I'd been completely forgotten by everyone, my spirits were sinking lower and lower, when a woman's light steps tapped rapidly to the door, and at last Matron appeared.

I'd prepared myself for some middle-aged disciplinarian, coldly antiseptic and hard as nails. What a pleasant surprise it was to see this smiling young woman, scarcely more than a girl, who at once took me in hand and, out of what was evidently much experience of lost, homesick youngsters, proceeded to cheer me up, while showing me my bed in the dormitory, and helping me unpack and put away my belongings. Young as she was, she possessed a mature assurance in dealing with those a few years younger than herself and soon made me feel more at home, raising the level of my morale, so that when a boy of about my own age entered the long room I faced him without nervousness as she introduced us, looking upon him as a potential friend.

He responded amicably enough; but he hadn't come, as Matron had anticipated, to take me down to evening assembly in Big Hall, where the public introduction of new boys always took place. Instead he informed her, with an embarrassed glance at me, that he brought a message from the Head; and the two of them retired to the passage, leaving me to listen to the murmur of their voices through the closed door and to wonder what the reason for this secrecy could be. In due course, Matron came back alone, and I thought her pleasant face wore a slightly worried expression, though she was as cheerful and friendly as ever.

I was delighted to be taken to her private apartment, adjoining the sick bay, considering myself fortunate to be sitting there eating ginger biscuits and drinking cocoa, instead of going through the alarming formality of being publicly presented to my future companions. I couldn't help being aware, however, that she was troubled and perplexed by this departure from immemorial custom, and her uneasiness gradually communicated itself to me, so that I ended by asking her why I hadn't been treated in the usual way.

She tried to pass it off by saying that it was probably because I'd arrived at half-term, instead of with other new boys when term began; the Head must have thought it would be embarrassing for me to stand up alone in front of the whole school, with nobody beside me. In view of what had occurred, unbeknown to her, in the Head's study, I thought such consideration for my sensibilities improbable in the extreme. And now I began to be faintly alarmed and to conjure up grim pictures of what this discrimination might portend.

None of the grisly possibilities I imagined actually came to pass. But I had to endure something more than coldness on the part of the other occupants of the dormitory, when I was finally left among them at bedtime. I thought they seemed an unfriendly, stand-offish lot but put it down to their annoyance at having to show me the ropes, according to Matron's instructions. It was some time before I found out what had happened at the assembly in Big Hall, from which I'd been excluded.

It was at these evening assemblies that the Headmaster made his most sensational and most weighty announcements. Only matters concerning the whole school were thus brought up and, by being so referred to, attained exceptional importance. So everybody was most curious to hear what he had to say that night.

Most of his hearers would know, he began, that a new boy was joining their ranks; a fact only deserving of notice because connected, in this case, with a secondary and sinister factor of the utmost significance. Never, in all the centuries of the school's existence, had there been any deviation from the principles laid down by the original founders, one of which was the Head's right to refuse admission to a pupil at his discretion. This right had now been summarily suppressed by a high authority he wasn't free to name, this same authority having enforced upon him the acceptance of the boy he'd just mentioned. To some members of his audience the boy's name might be familiar. It was a name which had been prominent in the press, receiving much publicity of widely different kinds. The boy's father had served his country well and this fact had been recognized, making his subsequent traitorous apostasy even more odious than it would otherwise have been. Admittedly, the son was not old enough to have participated actively in his father's guilt. But he'd been in intimate contact with loathsome doctrines, by which he must inevitably have been infected. Left to his own discretion, the Head would no more have dreamed of admitting him to the school than he would have allowed a known carrier of disease to mingle with his pupils. Authority had taken the matter out of his hands, forcing acceptance upon him with menaces, threatening dire consequences if the boy complained, either of the treatment he received here, or of disrespect to his father's name. In these circumstances, he had to forbid all reference to the man, and to enjoin upon them a distant attitude, flavoured with suspicion, towards the son. The principal felt that he could only keep his integrity by thus taking the whole school into his confidence, warning them solemnly of the danger in their midst, while relying upon their loyalty not to bring him into further conflict with those in power. He was sure they all shared his own horror of the doctrines with which the newcomer had been contaminated. It was his duty to remind them to be always on their guard, bearing in mind this infection carried within. Outwardly the boy was presentable; the impression he made was in some respects not unfavourable. Let them not be deceived by appearances, or his warning would have been in vain.

This speech was recorded in a volume the Head published some years later under the title 'Words and Warnings to Youth', from which I was able to copy it, and it explains much that was mysterious to me at the time. During my first term, while I was still unused to community life and everything still seemed strange, I was made most unhappy by the way my companions avoided me, despite all my efforts to please. Since I was, in spite of everything, a fairly normal young animal whose behaviour presented nothing unfamiliar to them, I think they'd have liked to be friendly. Some would even respond to my advances up to a point; but then, remembering the Head's warning, or reminded of it, would withdraw hastily in confusion, to my increasing bewilderment. I really began to think there must be something about me which prohibited friendship and that I'd lived too long alone ever to have any friends.

The following term my situation improved, mainly, I think, because it was summer, when a general tendency to relax is felt in our northern climate after the ice-bound winter and chilly reluctant spring. Having, presumably, got over the indignities he'd suffered on my account, the Head didn't repeat his warning. And as, with the passing terms, there was a larger and larger proportion of boys to whom his words were just hearsay, the memory of his speech gradually faded out: the whole affair slowly passed into a sort of legend, which finally even enhanced my reputation. Once I knew I had been accepted, and had firmly established myself, it rather gratified me to be pointed out as the villain of that old story.

Something had happened, nevertheless, in consequence of those lonely unhappy weeks I spent as a new boy, unaccountably shunned or, worse still, dropped abruptly after the first preliminary moves of friendliness. I myself was confirmed, once and for all, in the conviction that I was different from everyone else, unlovable and apart. And, whether because the distrust caution implanted in me made intimacy impossible, or for some other more obscure reason unknown to me, I never succeeded in making a really close friend. Being quite gregarious, and with a natural aptitude for all forms of sport, I wasn't unpopular; superficially I got on well with both boys and masters. But though I had hordes of acquaintances and was rarely alone, I remained isolated in spirit, incapable of, or reluctant to, embark upon intimate friendship. It was, with every potential friend, a case of so far and no further. A point quickly came beyond which the relationship would not, could not, advance. I didn't exactly want this to happen. But, as time went on, I accepted the pattern as inevitable and even took a sort of proud gloomy pleasure in the idea of walking alone in the midst of the crowd. All the same, I endured moments of near-panic, when I felt debarred from everything valuable and fated to be an outcast all my life.

At some point during my adolescence, I began to connect these fearful moments with a peculiar sense of vulnerability of which I'd become aware; an urgent need for protection, as though I'd been born minus some natural weapon everyone else possessed or were doomed to an unendurable fate nobody else would have to suffer. These irrational feelings were utterly real to me, the cause of much distress at this period, when for days at a time I was enveloped in nameless anxiety, of which I could speak to no one, from which I longed quite desperately to escape.

The unreal world, which used to lie so close behind the face of everyday things, had, since my coming to school, retreated further into the background, though I'd never lost touch with it altogether. So many exterior contacts had kept it in abeyance; I'd almost come to believe it was a part of the childhood I'd outgrown. Now, suddenly, I saw it as a way of escape, fulfilling my urgent need. Here was precisely what I wanted: a sanctuary always accessible to me but to no one else. Life might do its worst, if only I could elude it by taking refuge in another world where I was immune from pain. Unfortunately, the transition wasn't under my control. So I began to practise escaping, unfocusing my eyes, conjuring up a scene from memory or imagination and willing it to take the place of reality. I could never depend on being able to pass from one world to the other in this way at will. But I did, by degrees, attain some success in crossing the border-line. As may be imagined, opportunities for practice were few and far between in a life lived in close proximity to several hundred boys; and I had a dread of anyone finding out what I was trying to do, for it was clear to me that neither this form of escapism, nor the feeling that inspired it, could be considered quite normal.

So my experiments were mostly confined to the holidays, when I had all the solitude necessary and more. Taking a sandwich for my lunch, I would walk all day over our wild windy hills, without meeting anyone but a farmer, perhaps, out with his gun. Hill behind hill, the smooth curved downs were like the backs of a concourse of whales, swimming steadily past me on every side; for I seemed so close to the high white clouds, driven ceaselessly across the blue emptiness above, that everything around me appeared to be moving. I was alone, out of all creation, treading the turning globe, while the wind sang in the shells of my ears and thundered intermittently through the treetops of some wooded chine as I passed, constantly flattening the combed short green hair-like grass for my feet. I experienced such exhilaration then that the familiar world seemed magically extended; I felt the corridors of the universe about to open before me. And in this exalted state it was easy to accept my difference and to glory in it. Even after the authentic elation had passed, I could still acknowledge my peculiarity, not in bravado but as an essential factor, always to be taken into consideration.

The fantasy of the moving landscape and the expanding dimensions of the everyday world encouraged me to believe I was close to being accepted as a naturalized citizen of that other place, which would admit me as a refugee in flight from reality, in case of emergency.

My timeless walks, reaching out to the boundaries of infinity, may not have been the most normal of holiday occupations. But I had few alternatives. The children I'd known had all gone on to other schools, none of the boys attended the same exclusive, costly, remote one as I did, so that I'd lost touch with them all. My mother took little part, these days, in the social life of the neighbourhood and made no attempt to provide me with companions.

I didn't realize then that there was a special reason for her isolation, neither worldly enough, nor, I'm afraid, interested enough, to wonder why she rarely went anywhere or entertained anybody. Always inclined to solitude, she had taken little notice of the local people at any time. I was scarcely aware of her growing seclusion, which was obscured by the attentions of Mr Spector. His visits were now much more frequent: when I was home for the holidays he often took us to cinemas, restaurants, theatres in the nearby towns, so that on the whole our existence seemed livelier than before.

It was my life at school that absorbed me. The people with whom I spent three-quarters of my time were so much more real that the others seemed shadowy by comparison, and even he retired into the background. I still had a great admiration for him and discussed with him all my doings, but my impression was that he purposely refrained from influencing me during this period. While we were apart I would almost forget him; and, even when we came together again, he took care not to exert that extraordinarily powerful charm which had formerly held me spellbound.

If he was a shadowy figure to me, how much less real my mother appeared. Occasionally I had a revival of the tender feelings which preceded my first term; but the drifting process, begun long before, continued steadily, and she seemed to make no effort to stop it. If I'd had a close friend, I might have discussed his attitude to his family. As it was, I could only wonder how parents who sent their young children away at the most impressionable age, for ten years or so, and for nine months out of twelve, could possibly have a satisfactory relationship with them. The rejoicings at the end of term always struck me as a little false. Personally, I was much more relieved when the holidays were over and I could return from what was merely an interruption of the main stream of my life – and, to judge from the noisy ragging which was traditional on the opening day and to which the staff turned a blind eye, my sentiments must have been general and officially approved.

Though far from studious, I always managed to scrape through my examinations by last-minute cramming and in due course attained the dignity of the sixth form. Now I had only about another year of school life before me, terminating in the final and most important exam of all, on which much of my future depended, for directly afterwards I would be leaving.

It was, I remember, on the morning of the day I was made a prefect that I received a letter in a handwriting I didn't recognize; but, preoccupied by my new honour and its attendant privileges and duties, I found no time to read it till late afternoon, when I was sitting in solitary state in the study which from now on would be mine alone. Then it was as though I'd been innocently going about all day with a bomb in my pocket; for the letter was from my father, who had just returned, having discovered at last, on the other side of the world, the peaceful place for which he'd been searching so long and to which he proposed to transfer his family forthwith. The ship which had brought him would remain in port for ten to fourteen days, preparing for the return trip, and during this time he would wind up his affairs and make all arrangements to leave the country for ever.

The letter contained some obscure reference to the need for haste, which I took as signs of his aberration – that peace-bee which had suddenly started to buzz so disastrously in his bonnet – for this was a disaster to me, pure and simple. He ended by saying he hadn't yet had time to write to the Headmaster but would be doing so very shortly, and in the meanwhile I could show him this letter.

So the Head didn't know so far; that, to me, was the one spark of hope. I still had a few more hours in which to think, to extricate myself from what could only be regarded as a catastrophe. I'd almost forgotten my father after so long. Hearing nothing from him, even his name never spoken, I'd long since ceased to think about his return. As for the crazy notion of starting life over again in some distant land, I never had taken it seriously; yet here it was, not a dream-like possibility in the dim future but an immediate present crisis. More than anything, I think, I resented the abrupt arbitrary fashion in which I was to be uprooted, without being consulted, without even a chance to say what I thought of the uprooting. I wasn't a child now, to be swayed by the thrill of adventure and travel. Only too clearly I saw what I'd lose by this upheaval, which would make nonsense of the years I'd spent here and turn my hard-won certificates into so much waste paper.

I'd been looking forward to a foreseeable future, among the sort of people I knew, where my school background would give me – over and above my own achievements – a definite and accepted standing, the main object of the expensive education I'd received being to bestow on the recipient an inalienable reputation that would be his for life. Now all this was to be sacrificed to the whim of an eccentric, who, in the eyes of my associates, was a traitor as well. I might have been more tolerant had my father written affectionately; but the letter was quite impersonal, ending by telling me that, since I could do nothing to expedite our departure, I might as well stay where I was for the present.

I was still half stunned by the news when the small boy lately assigned to me as a fag in my new glory came in with another letter, which had come by a later post. The sight of this youngster inflamed my resentment still further. The coming year was to have been my reward for all that had been difficult in the past. During this last year of my school life, I should have enjoyed most of the privileges of an adult without the responsibilities; members of the sixth were near-fabulous beings to the junior school, respected, almost worshipped; from henceforth I had only to speak and people would fight to fulfil my wishes, my words would be listened to like those of an oracle, for my will was law. Whenever things had been hard during the long years, I'd comforted myself with the prospect of this idyllic period now opening before me. To have it snatched away at the very moment of attainment was bitter indeed.

I was in as black a mood as I'd ever known when I opened my mother's letter. She seemed almost panic-stricken at the idea of leaving home – why, I couldn't imagine; *she* had nothing to lose by the change. Her agitation annoyed me, for it seemed so pointless. And when she went on to say that my career would be ruined, bringing up all my own arguments, I felt she was only pretending to be concerned because she wanted my backing, being so disturbed on her own account. The one sensible suggestion the letter contained was that I should appeal to the Headmaster and get him to write to my father on my behalf. Of course, I couldn't possibly go to the Head; but, all the same, it wasn't a bad idea to get somebody to write.

Long before this, I'd heard all about the famous speech in which the whole school had been warned against me, and I still felt the hostility of the speaker; indeed, he made no secret of it and always took care to avoid any contact with me. Not once had he spoken to me personally in all the time I'd been here or displayed the least interest in anything I did.

My housemaster was the obvious person for me to consult; a good-natured, plodding, conscientious man, in no way remarkable, whose name I've even forgotten, though he was known as Jaggers among us. The events of the past had faded out of my memory, so that it was not till I was facing him at the interview I had requested that I recalled he was the very man who had witnessed my first encounter with the Head all those years ago. Now the details of the scene came back to me, but, humiliating as it had been for him, I was forced to refer to it when explaining how my father had gone away and left me in the lurch – I could only hope time had removed the sting from the insults he had received.

But clearly they'd been rankling ever since, and, though I tried to placate him by attributing Mr Spector's arrogant behaviour on that occasion to the effects of strain and the exhaustion of the long hours he had spent at the wheel, neglecting his work in the city to bring me here, taking over the duties my father had abandoned, he stopped me, exclaiming, 'Stop! I won't hear any more of this', starting to pace the room in considerable agitation.

He seemed to me quite absurdly upset; but what most dismayed me was his unmistakable antagonism, for which I could see no reason but the inevitable one, so that I blurted out reproachfully, 'You always sympathize with other people's troubles. But when I ask you to help me you get angry – you're against me like everyone else. And this is so important to me – it means my whole future. I did think that for once . . .' Ashamed of becoming emotional, I relapsed into silence. He seemed affected, even slightly embarrassed, by my outburst, for he stopped walking about and said in a more moderate tone, 'I would gladly help you, if I could be sure of not ruining myself in the process.'

I had expected him to contradict my statement that everyone was against me; but, though it surprised me that he let it pass, I was much more struck by his use of the word 'ruin', which sounded wildly extravagant in this context, almost suggestive of persecution mania. I'd often heard it said that old Jaggers had a screw loose. But when I thought of the Head's vindictiveness towards me, a private vendetta carried on over the years by an elderly scholar against a defenceless boy under his protection, Jaggers's fears seemed more justifiable, and I said impulsively, 'Is the Head really such a tyrant? Would he really take it out on you for helping me? Why has he always hated me so much?' I couldn't have asked these questions of anyone else, and I regretted my impetuousness in asking them now, though their effect was far from any I could have foreseen.

'The Head . . . ?' Jaggers stared at me with a bewildered expression, which changed quickly to one of incredulous excitement as he seized my arm, dragging me over to the light, and tilted my face up to scrutinize it minutely, muttering under his breath, 'Can it be true? Is it possible?' and similar expressions of wondering disbelief.

I never could stand being handled by people in this way, and Jaggers's mystification and his whole conduct were so peculiar that I was growing convinced I'd made a mistake in confiding in him. So I said nothing but disengaged myself as unobtrusively as I could, not wanting to offend him.

'And what about the authorities that sent you here?'

I was quite unprepared for the question, rapped out in his stern classroom voice, and it startled me, by recalling the Head's words, reviving suddenly my feeling of being exposed and somehow in need of special protection – a need which, since I'd reached the security of the sixth form, I'd almost forgotten.

However, I answered coolly enough, I believe, that I'd always assumed the Head's talk of authorities was meant to frighten ignorant little boys and that he might just as well have referred to the bogey-man. I smiled at the fantastic idea of important, powerful persons concerning themselves with my insignificant affairs; which left Jaggers no choice but to smile back. Pretending to believe I'd convinced him I was sincere, I began to thank him effusively, saying I was sure my father would be guided by his advice and experience both as a scholar and as a man of the world; flattery to which he succumbed, agreeing to write the letter, though he evidently had difficulty still in getting over his amazement, constantly interrupting himself with incredulous exclamations. 'All these years . . . how could I not have known?'

I was much relieved when the letter was finally finished. But, as I was leaving, he detained me at the door, giving me some very strange looks which I couldn't interpret and seeming to want to say something more; though he thought better of it in the end, and we parted without any further talk.

My father's reply came a few days later, a coldly worded note, stating briefly that he'd cancelled the reservations previously made and would wait for my return to discuss things more fully. I gathered that he was going ahead with the business of getting our passports and other necessary documents, so that the project was only postponed in his mind. On the other hand, he hadn't told the Head he would be taking me away at the end of the term; and I derived what comfort I could from this fact.

Jaggers's cooperation, seen retrospectively, didn't seem very wholehearted; I was faintly ashamed of having made use of someone I really rather despised, and if I'd followed my inclinations I would have had no more contact with him. But, in common politeness, I had to show him the letter; and I couldn't find any excuse for declining an invitation to tea. His teas, famous for their lavishness, were one source of the mild popularity he enjoyed, particularly among the juniors, and I remember this one because of the effort I made to disguise my lack of friendliness by a determined onslaught upon the cakes, scones, sandwiches, pastries and so on.

Though Jaggers positively radiated goodwill, this, too, seemed of doubtful spontaneity. I had the idea he had first to overcome some sort of constraint or discomfort, even dislike; so that our feelings for one another were very likely mutual. He had merely glanced through my father's note at the start without commenting on it. Presently he picked it up again from among the tea things and began to study it so minutely and for such a long time that (though I guessed he was only concealing the fact that his genial talk had run dry) I was impelled to ask what he thought of it.

I hoped he might have noticed some encouraging point I had overlooked. But he only added to the discomfort I already felt on this score by saying my father had evidently been terribly disappointed and it must have been a great blow to him that I didn't share his views. 'He's a good and brave man – even a great man; I'm certain of that.' Jaggers spoke the unexpected words with defiance almost, looking me straight in the face, as if waiting for me to contradict him (which I was much too taken aback to do) and adding still more vehemently, 'No one could have acted as he did without very great courage – heroic courage.'

I was most disconcerted; but not too much so to notice that he flushed slightly as he spoke and afterwards fidgeted awkwardly with his cup, seeming to wish he hadn't expressed himself so openly and emphatically before a critical – possibly even a hostile – listener.

I'd made no great effort, I had to admit, to overcome his distrust. But it caused me, all the same, to be overwhelmed once more by that frightening sense of being an outlaw, vulnerable beyond others, everyone's hand against me. And though the feeling was momentary, it left an aftermath of depression; and, as soon as was decently possible, I excused myself and prepared to leave. Jaggers came to the door with me, keeping me there as before; this time he did succeed in saying something, though with a curious shyness, looking aside, as if speaking to someone else. 'The greatest courage isn't always found on the battlefield, you know.' Observing him then, with his grizzled head and baggy grey tweeds, the gown he'd forgotten to take off hanging behind him like the dishevelled black wings of some great moulting bird, I dimly perceived that this mild, undistinguished, unprepossessing man knew a good deal about courage himself at first hand – which disconcerted me once again.

Kind and friendly as he had been, he'd somehow put me on the defensive. I felt that he criticized my attitude towards my father and probably regretted having helped me reveal it to him. So, though he'd pressed me to drop in for a chat, I never did, only seeing him in public till the term was almost at an end.

Prefects, naturally, were expected to set an example by being punctually in their places in Big Hall for the evening assembly. Jaggers's house where I lived was further than the rest from the main building, and, as I never started till the bell was ringing, I always had a last-minute dash across the chess-garden to be on time. No flowers grew here among the rows of tall evergreens, immensely old and cunningly clipped in the shapes of chessmen, by which I'd been so impressed when I first arrived. Even now, after years have passed, their weird aspect, hard and solid-looking as if carved out of malachite, is the thing I remember most clearly about the school. Only one man in the whole country was expert enough to give them their yearly trim, and his family had held the hereditary office since time immemorial. When the sun was high, these arborial curiosities could resemble a grotesque company of medieval giants, with their attendant dwarf-shadows. Or an army of green invaders from an alien planet sometimes seemed to be marching in ordered formation across the lawn, where only masters and prefects were allowed to tread. All their transformations, however, as my first glimpse had showed me, possessed the common quality of malice, which infected the air around them, as if, throughout the centuries of their long lives, they'd been accumulating contempt and bitterness for their human creators, which found expression in this emanation. As a new boy, looking out of the dormitory, I used to tremble at the sight of these spectral shapes, all looking towards me. Obviously, they knew all my secrets; they despised me and regarded me with suspicion, always wanting to trick and harm me, enveloping me in their malevolent influence. Later on, as I grew more sure of myself, the trees bothered me less. But I always thought of them as personifying derision and hostility; and I still felt an unacknowledged antipathy towards them.

On the summer's day I'm describing, my mind was occupied solely by the need for haste, as I was even later than usual. Swinging around one of the great green towers at full speed, not expecting to meet anyone here, where all sounds were muffled by the soft turf and dense compact foliage with its strange medicinal smell, I collided with someone I almost sent flying before I could pull myself up. Grasping his arms to steady him, I saw that it was Jaggers and gasped a breathless, 'Sorry, sir', inwardly cursing the unlucky delay. At this moment the bell ceased to ring. In the ominous hush I became aware of my victim's silence, then of his grey shocked face, which made me forget I was late and start asking anxious questions, afraid he'd been injured somehow by our collision. I felt, I remember, a curious pang of foreboding.

Waving a sheet of paper he held in his hand, he waved away my inquiries and instead put a question of his own – a question so extraordinary that I could scarcely believe my ears, hearing him ask the sailing date of the ship on which my father had first intended to leave the country. Amazed, I told him it should have sailed over a week ago. Whereupon he nodded slowly, a look of extreme anguish overspreading his face, and muttering, 'Yes, I thought so', in the way of a man overwhelmed by guilt, so that he might have been saying, 'Yes, it's all my fault.'

Though I had no idea what he meant, and was completely bewildered by the whole situation, for a moment he seemed to project his guilt on to me; as in a nightmare flashback I suddenly recalled with horror the guilty child whose imagination had once assumed responsibility for his father's fate. 'He's too late now,' I heard Jaggers murmur; but paid no attention to the words, too perturbed by his condition, convinced that he was wandering, temporarily out of his mind.

I tried to lead him towards the entrance of the main building. But he resisted, violently threw off my hand and, thrusting upon me the page he carried, covered his face with his hands and to my consternation began shaking from head to foot as if silently sobbing. I was thankful to catch sight of one of the gardeners who must have been working late, to whom I shouted, telling him to get help at once.

I'd noticed a seat at the edge of the topiarian chessboard and, thinking Jaggers would rest more comfortably there, tried to take his arm in order to lead him in that direction. But again he flung off my hand, which had barely touched his sleeve, as though it had been a repulsive snake. There was such violent loathing in this rejection that – though I knew how absurd it was to take offence at the actions of anyone in his state – I couldn't help feeling hurt and made no further attempt to come near him.

He continued to stand there, his face hidden, apparently

oblivious of me; and I presently glanced down automatically at the paper he'd forced me to hold. It was badly crumpled, the print blurred and almost illegible; I stared at it for some moments before recognizing it as a single news-sheet, roughly printed by some emergency process, which gave the news of the first of the sequence of big explosions which, in such a short time, laid waste our principal cities and came to be known as the Eight Days War.

In the confusion which followed immediately, a triviality like Jaggers's breakdown passed unnoticed. He simply disappeared, as so many people inexplicably appeared or vanished at this time, and was forgotten. Everything was chaotic, for the transport, postal and other services were at once out of action. It was impossible for us to be sent home. And, in any case, most parents presumably preferred to know that their children were in a place of comparative safety, far from any important centre. This remoteness was our most valuable asset, of great value, not only in ensuring our immunity from attack but because it permitted us to go on functioning as a closed, self-sufficient community – as we were able to do with our large home farm – without being immediately overrun by hordes of demoralized homeless people from the big towns.

These starving refugees from the shattered cities, many of them sick or with minds unhinged by suffering, flooding over the countryside in every direction, in lawless, leaderless, tragic mobs, were a problem as grave and were as much a cause of our country's final capitulation, as the actual bombs. Fortunately for us, they took some time to reach our remote peninsula, and, indeed, only a trickle ever survived the journey.

Whether the Head realized this danger on his own account or was warned of it by a higher authority, I don't know; but, in any case, his ruthlessness now proved invaluable for our salvation. Where a more humane man would have wavered, he held relentlessly to the only course possible if any of us were to survive, stamping out sympathy, decreeing that every applicant for food or shelter be turned away and instituting the severest penalties for disobedience. Foreseeing the possibility of desperate wanderers trying to break in by force, the eldest among us were organized in patrols, whose duty was to keep constant watch from the outer boundary walls, which fortunately were high and in good condition. We had also to be on the alert for soft-hearted weaklings within our midst, who, despite the stringent measures taken to prevent it, might secretly have admitted some of these people, whom we were told to regard not as human beings but as a plague-spreading menace, to be kept out at all costs. In the last resort, we were authorized to make use of the rifles of the Cadet Corps, for the issue of which I was responsible to some extent.

It was a strange situation for boys of our age, and I recall quite clearly the curious atmosphere, which, in its febrile excitement, seemed to reflect the unnatural heat of that summer weather. Day after day of blazing windless sun terminated in an accumulation of thunderclouds and the oppressive threat of a storm which never broke. And this atmospheric pressure, working on our nerves, augmented the tension. It was August, high summer; but with us such a stretch of unbroken heat is extremely unusual, especially in conjunction with the absence of wind, which greatly facilitated the accuracy of the bombing, so that rumours circulated to the effect that the weather was controlled by our enemies to their advantage and which, to us in our ignorance, seemed fantastic then. But it was hard not to imagine all sorts of weird happenings in that unnatural heat, which seemed to breed rumours like fever germs. I suppose it was inevitable, since we didn't even know whom we were fighting.

Though our generation had grown up with the idea of war as a background to life, and had been familiar with war from the cradle, we'd also inherited some respect for the old tradition of chivalrous warfare. We were acquainted with the theory that wars should be fought by professional armies, recruited voluntarily; that battles shouldn't involve civilians; that soldiers shouldn't fire on the Red Cross or on prisoners of war. Certainly, we ourselves had no experience of this gentlemanly style of fighting, but in most of us, I believe, the respect for it lingered on as a deep-rooted inheritance. I don't think a single one of us would, in a secret ballot, have voted for the slaughter of defenceless populations without means of retaliation, if only because this was against our schoolboy code of fair play. None of us had known this new modern type of bombardment, dependent for its success on the element of surprise, which automatically ruled out the old-fashioned declaration of war. Our country succumbed so quickly because it was the first to be taken by surprise in this way. We were the guinea-pigs of the world, which greatly profited by our experience; and we were hampered by being the last inheritors of the now obsolete idea of 'honourable warfare', unable to adjust ourselves fast enough to the new ideology.

But this is disconnected from the boy I was at the time, whose thoughts and feelings were still partially childish. I couldn't help thinking now and again what bad luck my father had had in returning from his long search for peace just in time for the most frightful war we'd ever experienced. If the thought of my own responsibility were anywhere in the background (as, after Jaggers's remarks, it seems that it must have been), my consciousness carefully censored it. There was no time for brooding over personal feelings, as everyone was immediately conscripted for some work useful to the community, in which I, as a prefect and member of the sixth, was expected to take a leading part. At first, the junior boys, and some seniors who should have known better, were in an excited state, apt to look upon this divergence from the norm as a sort of prolonged picnic. Such jobs as digging potatoes and even indoor chores seemed a pleasant change from ordinary classwork, especially as time off was allowed for games and swimming and resting from the hot sun. But, under our stern supervision, the febrile excitement which infected the youngsters, often making them obstreperous and hard to control, gradually subsided, and even they began to get some inkling of the seriousness of what was going on and to share the anxiety of their elders, many of whom were moody or depressed, disguising fears for their families under an assumed toughness.

Of course, I suffered like other people from these emotional disturbances, for which the heat seemed such a perfect breeding ground. I had no worries over my parents' safety, knowing our isolated cottage to be far outside any possible target area. But the old story of my father's switch to pacifism – which everyone else had most likely forgotten – revived in my memory and made me extremely touchy, imagining people suspected me of cowardice in consequence and only refrained from saying so because of the Head's words all that time ago. And I was impelled to disprove the unmade accusation by demonstrating my courage and militancy in various extreme ways.

For instance, I was the first to volunteer for the boundary

patrols, which soon came under my leadership altogether. And my repeated requests led to the issue of rifles from the Cadet Corps and to our being authorized to use them in case of need. Our instructions were, as long as ammunition was plentiful, to fire one preliminary warning shot, but if supplies dwindled this was to be dispensed with. Fortunately it never came to this; we never had to fire twice. But, whenever I handled a rifle, I felt guilty, wondering what my father would think if he knew I was quite ready to shoot to kill – and defenceless, starving people of my own country at that, whose only crime was their sufferings – and had persuaded or forced other boys to bear arms with the same object.

On the sixth day after the first bomb fell, rumours of an armistice became so strong that, though we were strictly forbidden to take any notice of such tales, one could hardly disregard them, especially since they didn't expire in the usual way to be replaced by others but persisted and strengthened as time went on. People were always asking me, in my capacity as patrol leader and prefect, whether there was any truth in the story; and they obviously remained unconvinced when I replied that I knew no more than they did.

All the next day the rumours went on. And the following day they were almost overwhelming, and all to the same effect. But I forgot them in my amazement at being sent for by the Headmaster, for the first time in the whole of my school career. On the way to his study, I was conceited enough to believe he might be going to congratulate me on my zealousness in patrolling the walls and maintaining discipline and morale, for I could imagine no other reason why he should want to see me.

But it was obvious as soon as I entered that his hostility

was unchanged. Barely glancing at me, he acknowledged my salute only with a curt nod, while he went on writing at his desk in front of the open window. Outside there, I could see the chessmen, at their most mocking, crowd one behind the other to peer in derisively at me, as though all the centuries-old malice, which should have been distributed over the whole human race, had been concentrated on me alone.

It shows how far from normal our reactions were at this time that I should have thought the man at the desk could be in league with these trees and had deliberately planned to subject me to the barrage of their spectral contempt. Though I looked away from the window and forced myself to keep calm, I became increasingly conscious of the uncanny disparagement out of doors, which, against all natural laws, reached me from a different category of existence, and I felt a fine perspiration break out on my forehead, though it was cool in the room.

Suddenly the Head looked up, fixed upon me an unrelenting gaze, without recognition, as if he'd never seen me before, and said in an icy voice, 'Your protectors have seen fit to inform me that an armistice has been signed. I shall give out the news at lunchtime. I was instructed to tell you privately to expect a visit sometime during the day. That's all. You may go.'

To my disorganized brain, the sight of his implacable face seemed like a confirmation of the triumphant philosophy of hate, already paramount in the world, and, though it registered the meaning of what he'd said, this for the moment was put aside, as, without a word, I saluted again and left the room. My equilibrium slowly returned as the distance increased between me and the remorseless antagonism of the man, so much older and wiser than I, who, after so many years, could still look upon me as an enemy and a stranger with such assurance of rectitude; but, still unable to face the antique deriding presences of the chess-garden, which I identified with him, I walked a long way round to my study and remained there in a very queer frame of mind till the bell rang for lunch.

The news of the armistice, as the Head gave it out, aroused very little excitement in his hearers, who had already, for the past week, been experiencing the maximum excitement of which they were capable. And, in any case, demonstrations of rejoicing, or even of relief, were forbidden. Our troubles, and those of our country, were far from over, he told us ominously; indeed, the worst might still be to come. There was to be no relaxation of the defensive measures we had adopted; so, when the time came, I went out with my rifle to patrol the wide boundary wall.

A part of my daily duty was to assign new stations to everyone there, on the assumption that the eye, growing accustomed to a particular view, transmitted to the brain a sense of familiarity, resulting in a slackening of the protective mechanism. Remembering the visitors I'd been told to expect, I myself took a position commanding an extensive view of the road, from the point where it left the forest borders and crossed the flat cultivated ground to our gates. The post happened to be one I hadn't occupied before; but the prolonged heat wave had given a depressing sameness to every vista, a barren brown lifelessness, the trees already autumnal, their leaves falling or turning yellow as if scorched by invisible flames. For the first time since the patrols began, I felt profoundly apprehensive; the appearance of a belligerent crowd, bent on vicious attack, wouldn't have been half so alarming as the prospect of this coming encounter with people unknown to me but doubtless connected with the 'authorities' of the Head's original oration. My recent interview with him, short as it had been, seemed to have resurrected and infused with new life obscure semi-superstitious fears of childhood I'd almost forgotten. Once more I felt vulnerable, lonely, outside the pale, as I'd done years ago; unfit to love or be loved, overshadowed by some obscure nightmare menace beyond my understanding. Deep within me, old remembered horrors opened their bleeding throats like wounds. The personality I'd built up through the years, the sixth-form prefect, confident and admired, on good terms with people, had been no more than a ghost, exorcized by a single glance. The Head's inexorable expression, his cold look that had turned me into an enemy stranger, had also made me a stranger to myself and to this world of school in which I'd believed I was at home. I was an intruder here; I had never been accepted. And now, looking back, I seemed to remember seeing similar hostile distrustful looks on many faces beside his. I remembered silences when I'd entered a room, topics suddenly dropped, because the speakers could not go on speaking freely before a stranger suspected of being a traitor.

If, as I half believed, the Headmaster was in spiritual communication with the green monstrous shapes outside his window, he must have been highly amused by the torment they'd devised for me between them, reducing me to the victim of childish terrors I'd thought I had long outgrown, as I waited, in fear and trembling, for the nightmare visitors I couldn't even imagine. Presently, shamed out of my abasement, I started to patrol the section of wall under my supervision, as each of us was supposed to do at least once while on duty; and the effort of keeping my balance exchanged occult fears for the more bearable fear of the laughter I should arouse by toppling into the currant bushes below or the nettles outside the wall. I had a few words with my next-door neighbour, who seemed gratifyingly friendly, and was feeling much more confident when I returned to my post.

Could the war really be over so soon? I wondered. So little did we know then of its horrors that it was possible for me, with childish autism, to regret the return of peace, which to me then meant only going back to my parents and all the business of our proposed departure that war had providentially shelved. I was so far from realizing the chaos into which the whole world had been thrown that, though vaguely envisaging some delay, I quite expected ships to be carrying passengers about the globe as before.

Noticing a change in the light, I looked up and saw that, as usual, the cloudless sky, out of which the sun had all day been blazing down, had grown overcast with the approach of evening. Very soon the sun would go down, which meant, as far as I was concerned, that it would soon be too late for visitors to arrive from the city. I started to feel relieved; then, to make sure nobody was in sight, carefully surveyed the stretch of country before me. Finding it empty, I again raised my eyes to the sky.

Every evening the same thing happened. Once again the great anthracite-coloured clouds had piled stealthily in the west. But now a change was occurring: a few thin unexpected rays fanned out above and sprayed the vacant landscape with their expiring light, a weird radiance in which details emerged with a trick-like strangeness, as if flood-lit.

Nothing about the view had as yet actually changed; the grey-black head of cloud still obscured the sky, wearing its rayed diadem; the drab stretch of country, the thinning trees, were just the same. Only the solid permanence of reality seemed to have gone and with it all that made sense to my understanding – the reliability of appearances on which sanity depends. It can't be real, I thought blankly, staring at the approaching car like an hallucination. Already within our gates, it came in a cloud of yellowish dust along the road just below me at a speed that must have made it difficult for the occupants to distinguish between the young figures posted along the wall. On it came unhesitatingly, to stop directly beneath the spot where I stood.

Simultaneously the descending sun reached a crack between cloud and horizon and through this narrow aperture, to my confusion, hurled its last light in a lurid flare, distorting everything, and falsifying proportions, so that for a moment I seemed to see the world through the eyes of a child on a bank, apprehensively looking down at the great black beetle-like car filling the narrow lane, a queer medicinal scent teasing my memory with its elusive association – before I could catch it, three people got out of the car now below me.

This was certainly a mistake. There ought not to be three, I wished to protest. One of them I knew I should recognize; I *did* recognize Mr Spector, though he seemed different in some way, strange. Before I'd decided what was strange about him, his accustomed appearance reassembled itself, the two superfluous armed figures ceased to perplex me, I was dazzled no longer. Suddenly I saw my surroundings real, concrete again, in dun-coloured dusk; while, apparently dissociated from everything and instantly lost, the thought came to me that the child I'd once been wasn't yet so completely forgotten that he could be considered dead.

The sun had set now. All unreality and distortion ended, I once more stood on the wall in my proper self, looking down at my old friend and his armed escort.

Of course it was Mr Spector, I thought, jumping down and hurrying through the currant bushes with outstretched hand. What a perfect fool I'd been to imagine anyone else could conceivably be the first to reach us with news from outside. My old belief in the man's infallibility had returned, and I felt drawn most warmly towards him. My childish fears now seemed utterly ludicrous. I was so happy just to see him again that I found myself saying, 'How splendid of you to come.'

He didn't seem surprised at this unusual display of boyish enthusiasm on my part, accepting it, as he accepted my hand, with a faint enigmatic smile. Yet I wasn't disappointed: this was his most attractive, most benevolent self; there was no need for him to say anything; it was as if he exuded good-will, convincing me, without a word or a sign, of his unchangeable friendliness.

Though I'd drifted away from him during recent years, as I had from my mother, allowing the world of school to absorb my emotions as well as my interest, I'd always remained aware of his ultimate importance to me, which was, in changing circumstances, the one unalterable certainty. I knew now that the years between didn't matter, our intimacy being established upon a plane unaffected by temporary ups and downs. Impulsively I started questioning him about the course of events, but he silenced me by a gesture, told one of his attendants to take my place on the wall and returned to the car, signing to me to follow. As I obeyed him, a faint sense of repetition touched me with the eerie proximity of long-forgotten events, as though the past was gathering around us in the dusk. Then, banishing all such imponderables, Mr Spector asked where we could talk without danger of interruption, and I directed him to drive on a little way to the enclosed rickyard, to which nobody ever came at this hour.

His wish for privacy rather surprised me. But I felt no

apprehension, looking at him with implicit trust, waiting for him to speak. It was years since I'd felt this particular sort of warm, confiding affection that made me eager to do whatever he asked, without question, to throw in my lot with him, without reservation of any kind. I'd almost forgotten that he could be so endearing at times, so that his goodwill seemed more valuable than anything in the world.

Looking back from this distance of time, I've no doubt whatsoever that he knew exactly what I was feeling and quite likely had induced me to feel as I did, for he kept his eyes on me all the time, turning sideways to do it and leaning against the window, his arms lying across the wheel, his long legs stretched out across mine. It was getting darker each moment, but a lingering gleam of sunset was on his face, enabling me to distinguish the piercing brightness of his eyes and his fixed expression, which combined sadness with affection. To my surprise, his large, cool, powerful hand closed over my own, pressing it encouragingly for a second before he said, 'I've brought you bad news, Mark, I'm afraid – the worst possible news.'

His voice was melancholy, grave and sincere. I couldn't doubt that he meant precisely what he'd just said. But the strength of my personal feeling for him – or, if you like, of his influence over me – transcended everything else. I was neither alarmed nor especially curious about his news. The simple fact of sitting here beside him was far more important, enclosing me in happy serenity and security, safe from all my former agitations and fears.

I couldn't bear to interrupt this peaceful happy intimate moment. It was one of those moments of conscious respite and relaxation, made more poignant by the knowledge of coming trials, that one longs instinctively to extend into infinity. However, I knew I must resist the temptation to abandon myself to it, and, returning with an unwilling effort to world affairs, asked naïvely, 'Have we lost the war?'

'That, too.'

In strange contrast to my own almost indifferent question, the two words, heavily spoken with a dying fall, sounded so ominous that I was startled at last. They pointed clearly to some other disaster, concerning me more directly; but what catastrophe could have occurred grievous enough to merit that gloomy tone or to be mentioned in the same breath as a nation's fall?

'My father . . . ?' Once my thoughts had turned in the direction of pacifism they began running away with me, imagining all sorts of disturbing eventualities. Perhaps he'd led hostile demonstrations against the authorities; perhaps he'd spoken in public against the war, trying to convert people to his own views; perhaps he'd engaged in subversive activities (whatever *they* were); perhaps he was to be put in gaol or even shot as a traitor . . .

'He was caught on the first day, by the first bomb.'

This quiet statement arrested my sensational guesses and covered me with confusion and shame. I was thankful there wasn't enough light to reveal the flush I could feel on my cheeks as guilt and remorse overwhelmed me. How could I have been thinking these shameful thoughts about my father, who had suffered an experience so horrific I couldn't even begin to imagine it? Suddenly it struck me that even now I wasn't thinking of him but always of my own reactions and feelings. Such egotism really dismayed me; and, to escape from it, I asked quickly and without thinking what I was saying whether he had been injured.

'Killed.'

The shock of the single crude word hit me like a stone. Involuntarily I winced and shuddered, taking it as either a reproof or an accusation, assuming that Mr Spector was aware of my heartless thoughts. Immediately afterwards I found myself thinking: Of course; as though my father's death were inevitable and I'd known for a long time that it would happen like this. Yet, at the same time, I knew I hadn't grasped it so far as an actual fact, and the two conflicting ideas confused me. What was I supposed to do or say now? I was aware of having been silent too long already, but no suitable words came to me. I tried out one or two sentences in my head and rejected them as inadequate.

'You remember I said it was *the worst possible* news?'

The emphasis, the heavy significance, of this was unmistakable. But though some part of me seemed to understand it, my muddled brain couldn't find the meaning, or didn't want to. However, I was to be given no choice in the matter; I was to be forced to understand, whether I liked it or not. I felt I was being driven into a trap but could only resign myself to the insistence of my companion's will by asking, 'What else has happened?'

'He was not alone.'

No doubt this was kindly meant, an attempt to break it gently. But in my bewildered state I was completely baffled by the words 'not alone', which conveyed nothing to me. Perhaps my slowness roused Mr Spector's impatience, or perhaps he decided it would be kinder to tell me the worst at once. At all events, he went on, 'Your mother was with him. She complained of having been left alone in the country for so many years and said she wanted a little gaiety for a change. So your father took rooms at a hotel for a few days. They must have been on their way to a theatre . . .'

The low flat voice, a sign, though I didn't know it, of the speaker's profound emotion, ceased rather abruptly. I took no notice of it, still half dazed and surprised by this last item of news. Had she, too, been hurt? I asked, not realizing the absurdity of the question, though something unnatural about his muted assent began to sound the alarm. 'Not . . . ?'

Those younger than ourselves must find it hard to understand, with their direct approach to death, the taboos with which we hedged it round, not yet able to accept it as a commonplace of our lives. It wasn't emotion that inhibited me from speaking the word 'killed' but the feeling that it sounded melodramatic, sensational, incompatible with everyday matters, almost in bad taste. But Mr Spector, whose intellectual equipment was far in advance of mine, felt no such inhibition and said with a direct simplicity that ought to have braced me, 'They both died instantaneously.'

I tried in vain to assimilate this, revolving the words in my mind. No, it was no good. I couldn't take it in. Silently, with the distant vagueness of a patient coming out of an anaesthetic, I watched him switch on a small light in front of us, producing from somewhere a paper parcel, which he proceeded to unwrap, saying as he did so, 'I'm sorry about this, Mark. I hate to distress you. But no one else can give the identification the authorities need.'

Without in the least understanding what he meant, I felt a far-off tremor of warning, gazing blankly at the oddly shaped object he held out for my inspection. The queer-looking incomplete thing, with its charred irregular edges and tapered projection, seemed faintly reminiscent of something I couldn't recall. I told him I didn't know what it was, wishing he'd put it away. As the seconds passed, I was developing an unreasonable aversion towards the nameless fragment, more particularly to its smell; for it gave off a peculiar odour I'd never before encountered – an acrid chemical smell, mixed with the smell of old burnt material and something bitter, heavy, oppressive, which I couldn't place and which yet seemed familiar. This composite odour was strangely penetrating, clinging and disagreeable, pervading the whole interior of the car; I felt it would hang about me for days if I touched the thing. Nevertheless, I was obliged to overcome my reluctance and take it into my hand, since it was held out inescapably. Still I could make nothing of it. I noticed the charring wasn't new; it seemed unnatural for the smell to cling so persistently. Vaguely turning it over, I discovered some rubbed gilt lettering, blackened and blurred at one end to illegibility but with the initial F still visible and guessed rather than saw an R and a G, puzzling over some lost association.

Then suddenly it came back. The shoes, neatly paired in their boxes, were strewn around us, prettily cuddled up side by side in their tissue beds. My mother's foot on the stool looked naked and unprotected in the thin stocking, till the assistant fitted on the soft elegant suede, smoothing it tenderly around the ankle. 'Ferragamo. I always wanted a pair. But they're so expensive. Do you think I'm terribly extravagant, Marko?'

The shoe shop faded. I was left with a sinking premonition of similar visions to come, remembered incidents of no importance, trifles, perhaps irritating at the time but, in retrospect, of an unbearable pathos. Still I could think of no appropriate words but, as I had to say something, said stupidly, 'They were her best shoes', and, to my own astonishment, burst into tears as if I'd been six years old.

I suppose Mr Spector took the remains of the shoe away from me then, for I remember hiding my face in my hands and being unable to find my handkerchief; he was very patient and kind, pushing his own into my fingers and letting me cry on his shoulder. And I remember how, momentarily, I seemed to recapture the heavenly peace of some remote childish occasion when I'd rested against him in this same way and lost it again at once, like a face seen from a fast-moving car.

I didn't feel anything much about my parents. I didn't even know why I was crying and felt ashamed of my tears, but I couldn't control them – they simply went on and on, for no reason. When they finally stopped, and I sat up, blowing my nose, I couldn't look at the man beside me, who said kindly, 'I'm afraid I have to go back now. Is there anything you want to ask me first?'

I felt I ought to ask questions about how my parents had died. But the only thing I wanted to know was whether this fragment of shoe was all they'd found of my mother – as he'd suggested by his words about identification – and this I couldn't bring myself to ask. I wondered if he'd be shocked by my selfishness when I said, 'Shall I have to leave now?' After all, I had to know what was going to happen to me.

The question seemed to surprise him. He told me that I must, of course, stay on and take the final examination, and we would see then what was to be done. 'And now I really must get back to my work.' After this broad hint, I said a hurried goodbye and got out of the car quickly, for something in his voice pierced my self-absorption, conveying an impression of the quite extraordinary importance of this work, the exact nature of which had never been revealed to me.

It had become quite dark. There was a moon, but only dim, intermittent gleams penetrated the heavy cloud. When the headlights came on I stepped back quickly out of their searchlight beams, surprised to see one of the soldiers getting into the back seat – had he been watching us all the time? The car swung slowly around and swayed out of the yard, bumping over the hollows, and I followed it but then turned the opposite way, not wanting to meet anyone, not wanting to go indoors. And I remember stumbling about aimlessly for a while, feeling sorry for myself, till I walked into a bush, which scratched my face and hands viciously.

The thorny scratch coming as a sharp reminder, I suddenly realized how I'd taken it for granted that Mr Spector would look after me, though he was under no sort of obligation to do so and obviously overloaded already with heavy responsibilities. It had seemed to me such a matter of course that I hadn't even thanked him. All my feelings of inferiority revived at this instance of my own graceless behaviour. No wonder people disliked and distrusted me; how could I ever have believed anything different? Even the death of my parents meant nothing to me, I thought, trying to evoke the scene before my imagination but defeated at the start by not knowing how they had looked. True, I knew my mother had been wearing her best shoes, but I couldn't remember her dresses well enough to know which she would wear to the theatre – most likely she'd bought a new one for the occasion, and this I couldn't possibly imagine. As for my father, I didn't get as far as trying to picture him, before the moon escaped abruptly through a ragged hole in the clouds, as though it had gnawed its way out.

In its pallid light, I saw that I'd wandered back unknowingly to the school buildings; I watched them glide, stealthy black masses, into the lighter space where just now only the night had been. For an instant then the horrors of all my childish nightmares were thick about me: tall spectres, petrified in innumerable malign mutations; and one calamitous shape towering above them all, as hideously unnatural as a child's control of a father's fate.

If I hadn't opposed his wish, he and my mother would be

alive now. So I'd killed him – killed them both. The thought I'd unconsciously been repressing since I'd heard the news at last thrust itself forward. Now the moon dimmed again, the phantoms blurred and were reabsorbed into darkness, stuff of darkness themselves. I repeated to myself, 'I've killed them both'; and the words 'So what?' followed closely enough to deprive the thought of all reality. I would keep it that way, unreal; my instant decision reduced the fact to the region of childish fantasy. Turning my back on the invisible chessmen, I cautiously moved away, my hands outstretched like a blind man's before my face, my fingers touching now close-clipped leaves, now the unevenness of old brickwork, now the cooler, smooth face of stone.

I was approaching Jaggers's house, when the picture I'd failed to create formed of its own volition; my mind's eye saw a city street, traffic and many people, everything shifting, confused, where my parents walked side by side among all the rest, unprotected and unsuspecting. To my callow youth, the pair looked elderly, almost old, and this, for some reason, gave them a curious air of innocence, pathos. And here the vision seems not incorrect; for they indeed belonged to the last of the innocents, of the trusting ones, who trusted their fellows as no man, perhaps, will ever trust others again.

So, thanks to Mr Spector, I didn't lose that last year at school as a senior and a prefect, which had seemed so desirable to me beforehand. Only, as is the case with so many things to which one looks forward in this life, the reality failed to come up to my expectations.

The old order of things had dissolved in chaos, from which the new had yet to emerge. Even our enclosed community was affected by the general disorganization and flux; the giants of the sixth form could hardly keep their traditional majesty when, in the outer world, so much tradition was being discarded. No one quite knew what the future would be. And for those of us who were soon to leave school, this presented a serious problem. No one wanted to waste time preparing for a profession that might be scrapped altogether or radically reformed. Instances of this sort of thing weren't uncommon and had an unsettling effect.

The Head, in what has since become one of his best-known speeches, advised us, with cynical common sense, to stick to those callings for which there was bound to be a demand in all circumstances. But none of the enumerated occupations appealed to me, such aptitude as I possessed lying in the direction of the arts, though I'd never had any clear-cut ambition to reach a particular goal. My vague literary and artistic leanings weren't strong enough to with-stand the demoralizing uncertainty of this final year, which ought to have given definition to my studies but actually had the reverse effect, leading me to the choice in the last examination of subjects which were non-committal, directed towards no special career.

Naturally, I'd been wanting all the time to discuss this subject, so important to me, with Mr Spector; but no opportunity had ever seemed to arise. Though he always arranged to see me during the holidays, he let me know he did so with difficulty, hinting obscurely at new powers and duties continually heaped upon him. Why didn't I take him up on these hints? I was to wonder later. It would have been easy then for me to find out his position, which was certainly high, for, as long as there was any risk of trouble in isolated parts of the country, he was accompanied by an armed escort wherever he went. But I'd always avoided personal subjects with him, and I thought it would look odd if I started asking him questions now, for the fact was that I could no longer feel myself his close friend. For this reason, too, I disliked the idea of making demands on his time. I had hoped he would appoint himself my official guardian after my parents' death. But, as the weeks went by and he made no move to define our mutual relations, I'd been forced to realize he had no such intention and that the position was to be left vague, which had distressed me so much that I think it may even have caused my inability to decide on a profession. Each time we met, I'd tried my hardest to win from him some sign of his former warmth; but, as nothing approaching intimacy or affection ever developed, I began to think I must have displeased him (though I couldn't imagine how) or that he'd taken a dislike to me and only continued to befriend me in this somewhat impersonal way for the sake of the dead.

It was a very unhappy position for me, for I still had a child's need to attach myself to someone; or, rather, I felt I *was* already irrevocably attached to him, whether or not he had any use for me. I had done unexpectedly well in the last examination, but I remember thinking as the term ended that nobody cared what became of me and that my future outlook was pretty grim.

Relentless to the last, the Headmaster didn't send for me before I left for the usual farewell talk. It didn't worry me; but I hoped he wouldn't refuse to shake hands with me in front of the others when we filed past for the final leave-taking. Looking straight into his cold arrogant face when my turn came, I noticed the slightly raised eyebrows, the glance at my outstretched hand; really I didn't see how he could avoid taking it. But, instead, he chose from a table beside him one of the gilt-edged books bound in tooled leather that were distributed as prizes, placing it in my hand and faintly inclining his head, turning it then to the next boy and leaving me to pass on; which I did without looking at him again. Now that it had happened, this little incident for some reason rather encouraged me, and I felt almost as though he'd paid me a compliment with an enmity so enduring.

I seemed to get the better of the chessmen, too, in the end. When I looked at them for the last time from Mr Spector's big car, they at first appeared utterly indifferent to my departure, standing stiff and unmoving in sombre rows. Then suddenly, on this bleak and blustery day, the wind set them confabulating; putting their black heads together, they gobbled and gabbled in growing excitement and finally started to dance up and down, as if in rage at being rooted there and unable to follow me, except with their clamorous mocking voices, whistling derisively after me as we drove away.

But these were transitory moments of exhilaration. As we passed through the tall gates, and the school and its grounds were left behind, I seemed only now to realize fully that I should never set eyes on the place again. Now that, like childhood, schooldays had gone for ever, the terms, which had seemed so long while I was living through them, appeared to have flashed past like express trains. Again I was moving into the future before I had even got used to the past. Would I never catch up with myself – must my whole life be spent in chasing a ghostly entity I could never grasp? I saw in my mind a small ghost, its hair flying about its transparent head, blown like an insignificant shred of thistledown over a dark ominous continent that was my precarious future. Filled with foreboding, I glanced at the granite profile beside me and thought it might have belonged to a stranger.

Mr Spector interrupted my thoughts with an unexpected question. 'Would you like a cigarette?' Holding the wheel with one hand, he flicked open his case with the other and held it towards me in a gesture he had never made before; it promptly assumed symbolic significance, marking my entry into the adult world. Next he wanted to know what my plans were, continuing, after I had answered evasively, 'I've been hoping you'd work for me.'

Even now I couldn't bring myself to ask the question that was on my mind; but perhaps he guessed it, for he said, 'I'm interested in so many concerns that I always need new assistants. You needn't worry about qualifications as long as you're prepared to work hard. The salary would be small at first. You'd have to work your way up from the bottom. But I could provide you with living quarters, which means a lot these days, as you'll see for yourself. You'd be perfectly independent, of course; your obligations to me would be the same as to any other employer, no more and no less.' He turned his head for an instant to look at me directly, and I felt the old spell of his power over me, catching, like a gleam of sunshine, the flicker of his attractive smile. 'I mean that you needn't be afraid I'd intrude on you in any way. My only stipulation is that you don't share the flat with anyone else. It's in the commercial district, you see, where no members of the general public are supposed to live. I've arranged things with the authorities as far as you're concerned, but they won't stand for another person living there. But don't decide in a hurry. I'd like you just to keep my offer in mind and we'll talk it over again later on, when you've had time to look around.'

In response to this suggestion my spirits immediately rose; because of that friendly smile, I felt happier than I'd felt for some time, convinced on the spot that to work for

Mr Spector in any capacity would be the most satisfying, indeed the only satisfactory career possible for me. Impulsively I jumped at his offer, saying I needed no time to think about it but would like to accept there and then.

'I'm glad you react in such a positive way,' he said, evidently gratified by my enthusiasm, 'though I shan't hold you to the bargain if, after you've been in town a few days, you come across something better.'

Needless to say, nothing better did turn up during the week or so Spector wished me to take as a holiday and to 'get my bearings'; a period of enforced leisure I'd have much preferred to forgo. This wasn't my first visit to the city; I'd already been here several times in the holidays and knew my way about. But I'd never been so much alone here as I was now, Spector being busy with his mysterious exacting affairs, leaving me to my own devices.

My impressions were confused and rather unfavourable. The work of building and demolition going on all around was too noisy for my country-bred ears. By day the incessant hammering was more insistent than the noise of the traffic; and at night it kept me awake, till I got used to it, and to the great livid floodlights in which tiny insect-like figures swarmed and scurried about or appeared solitary and outlined against the night sky, incredibly manipulating some mammoth machine.

Not knowing what to do with myself, I passed much of the time aimlessly wandering about, waiting for evening, when I might or might not see Spector again. He was the only person I spoke to, apart from the staff of the hotel at which he'd installed me; for, though I'd been to see several people I'd known at school, nothing had come of these visits and I didn't repeat them, feeling at a disadvantage without the established family backgrounds and safe futures my schoolfriends enjoyed. They, I'm sure, were puzzled by my different circumstances, unable to understand how a fellow 'old boy' came to be in such a position that he couldn't even return their hospitality – for I had neither the necessary assurance nor the money to invite them to the hotel. Too late, I realized I should have kept away till I was firmly established with a flat and a job of my own; till then they'd inevitably look upon me as potentially dangerous and likely to ask favours, identifying me with all that was alien to them and outside their way of life.

Seeing them so obviously sure of themselves, and of their world, I couldn't help envying, though I despised myself for it, the security they took for granted and the assurance I only tried feebly to imitate. Inaction became intolerable; I couldn't wait to start work and in my impatience prevailed upon Spector to let me curtail my holiday and begin at once. Before consenting, he repeated his warning that I would probably find the work dull and unworthy of my capabilities. Was I sure I had given the matter enough thought?

In fact, I'd hardly thought about it at all, taking it to be settled, as though it were impossible even to consider another job. Yet I've no doubt I could, at that time of depleted manpower, have obtained a post quite easily for myself, on the strength of my educational background alone, and it strikes me as strange now that I never made the slightest effort to do so during those long days of boredom, if only to pass the time that hung so heavily on my hands. Partly, I suppose, it was due to my diffidence, as I had no idea how to go about it and didn't like to ask. But I think it was even more the result of my dependence upon the man who had dominated me as long as I could remember, frightening and fascinating me by the two sides of his nature. That he had withdrawn himself from me to a great extent lately in no way lessened his power over me, an inscrutable influence from which I had no wish to escape. On the contrary, feeling insecure and alone in the world, and hurt because he hadn't identified himself with me more closely when my parents were killed, I was desperately anxious to attach myself to him now at all costs. His offer of employment suggested, to my wishful way of thinking, an advance on his part, and I hoped an improvement in our relations would follow. Even at this age, I must have been a good deal like a lost friendly pup, coming up again and again, tail wagging, longing to become the master's devoted slave, blind to the fact that it isn't wanted. Such an attitude was understandable, perhaps, just now, when I was particularly alone, starting a new life, in circumstances that seemed strange and unsympathetic. Everything would come right, I thought; I'd be able to settle down contentedly once I was working for him.

I imagined I would see more of him, and this gratified me as much as the chance to prove my loyalty, for I still derived the same pleasure from his proximity as when I was a child. I was so much under his spell again that if he'd set me to scrubbing floors I believe I would have been happy to do so. At all events, I was more than satisfied to find myself one of several junior clerks in an office in the tall building in which I was to live, which belonged to him, like the business.

As for the flat, I was delighted with this, my first home of my own, consisting of two attic rooms and the usual 'offices'. Not only was it a perfectly adequate bachelor apartment but it had a certain character, even charm, owing to the odd slope of the walls and ceilings and the wonderful views from all the windows. Spector had installed only the minimum of furniture, leaving me to add such decorative touches as I fancied and could afford. But all essentials were there, and the rather austere effect of the bareness pleased me. With no distractions inside, the eye was drawn at once to the view framed by each window, which was given a certain unreal romanticism by the height of the building, all that was shocking and ugly invisible now, the ruins dignified as relics of antiquity. Best of all, a door had been fitted at the top of the stairs, shutting off my domain from the storerooms and offices of the lower floors. Once this door was shut I was alone in my kingdom and, separated by six flights of stairs from the busy street life below, could sit and dream peacefully at the window, withdrawn from everything but the passing clouds and the pigeons strutting along the ledge.

My work, as I'd been warned, was uninspiring and easy; but the novelty of it and my own conscientiousness made this unimportant. I was proud of my new status as a wage earner; only disappointed to find I was not, after all, to be directly in contact with Spector. However, he came along to introduce me to the manager, assured me of his continued personal interest and promised to visit me as often as possible; and with this I had to be content.

Again I was impressed, as I had been at the hotel, by the extreme respect everyone showed him, which strengthened my conviction that he must be a very important person indeed, holding some influential position over and above the controlling interest in this and various other firms. Not to know what it was seemed too idiotic – incomprehensible really and barely credible, even to me. But I could not ask anyone about it, partly because my own feelings forbade it and partly because the attitude of my colleagues was unresponsive and aloof. This was a second grave disappointment to me. As much the youngest of them, fresh from school and utterly inexperienced, I'd expected to receive at least tolerant treatment, for I'm certain I gave no trouble to anyone, being industrious and most willing and never needing to be told anything twice. Indeed, the work was so elementary that I picked up all I needed to know in the first few days and thereafter saved the rest of them considerable labour by taking over much that they ought to have done.

But, though I was always polite and obliging, they showed an unfriendliness I could only attribute to the interest Spector had showed in me, assuming that they were jealous. The only other explanation I could think of was one I always tried not to contemplate: the old theory that something 'different' and unlikeable about me would always prevent me from having friends. But the recurrence of this childish pattern was disturbingly obvious in the conduct of those around me, who took advantage of my industry and good nature while indicating that they despised me for these qualities.

'You can't buy our friendship by doing our work,' they seemed to sneer, when, thanks to my help, they were able to rush away, leaving me alone in the deserted building. At times I thought I could actually see the contempt in their eyes when I handed over a pile of papers I'd dealt with for them, as much as to say, 'The more fool you for having done it.'

Loneliness, no doubt, made me unduly conscious of their behaviour. It was my first term at school all over again. No one responded to my overtures; no one spoke a friendly word; though, among themselves, they talked and joked like any group of lively young fellows. Only I was simply left out of their conversation – out of everything – ignored, as if I'd committed a crime.

To withdraw into myself was the only possible course open to me, and after a time I ceased to approach them, working silently at my desk, almost as much alone in their midst as I was in my flat upstairs, where I sat for hours on end, dreaming, resorting once more to that other world which was so much more dependable than the real one. In my daydreams I was no longer a lonely, unhappy, insignificant clerk in a city office but the hero of some sombre and tragic story, triumphing over all obstacles.

But a fantasy life, no matter how vivid, can't last all around the clock. During work hours I became like all the other insignificant, impecunious young men thronging the streets, the cafés, the restaurants; yet painfully aware that I was different from them, my singularity underlined every evening when they jammed the streets in home-going crowds, which gradually thinned until, when the places for eating and entertainment closed down, I was the only person left except for police and builders – in this area where private individuals were not allowed to have homes.

The jealousy and ill feeling of my colleagues became comprehensible when I got to know more about the frightful ordeal of finding somewhere to live, which played so prominent a part in their lives and from which Spector's influence had saved me. I couldn't possibly blame them for envying me my conveniently situated flat, when they had to travel long distances twice daily. How could they be expected to refrain from jealousy when I had two rooms all to myself – I, a mere schoolboy no one had ever heard of – while older and far more deserving people, some of them even actually famous, couldn't find a corner to call their own?

To make matters worse, there was now one of those sudden incomprehensible changes of policy to which our rulers are prone: suddenly it was announced that no more large-scale building projects would be started and of those already under construction only such as were needed for official purposes would be finished, so that private people could look forward to no improvement at all in their position.

Instead of the busy anthill appearance the city had worn since my arrival, it now promptly took on a deserted air, as the cessation of the perpetual hammering left an uneasy hiatus in our ears, which the noise of traffic couldn't entirely fill. This official policy of inaction, of course, had a bad effect on my own situation, as it did on public morale. I noticed an increased hostility in the office; as once before, I began to suspect sudden silences when I came in; my help was only accepted mistrustfully and with reluctance; and I became quite miserable, once more convinced that I was an outcast, hated by everybody. Above all, I was distressed by thinking Spector, too, must dislike me, otherwise he would never have placed me in this invidious position; and I went so far as to see, in the coldness with which I was treated, a projection of his own animosity. My attic home, once a source of such pleasure, turned into a burden – a handicap I'd have gladly exchanged for a little kindness. And now, just when I felt most wretched, the world of imagination, too, failed me as a way of escape, for I carried about with me always the tension accumulated in the office, which I was quite unable to shake off.

I remember an especially harassing day, when a rumour was circulating to the effect that the authorities had stopped building operations because a new catastrophe was known to be imminent. Looking at the resigned, despondent faces around me, I thought of my father's belief that, to a sane, healthy mind, war was an evil within man's power to avert, not the inevitable accompaniment of progress it was now supposed to be. Applying this, as I did every thought, to my own problems, I reflected upon the impossibility of normal thinking, when one was denied (like the majority of the population) the first essential of civilized life – the secure private retreat called a home of one's own. No wonder the housing question had acquired its almost metaphysical aura, when it dominated and distorted people's lives and thoughts.

Gradually my ruminations had been infiltrated by awareness of something which now interrupted them altogether: a peculiarly oppressive silence had fallen upon the office. Looking up quickly, I saw that all the others had stopped working and were looking at me in silence. I was quite used to their surreptitious glances; but this open concerted stare was something new; and I noticed that, as if by some sinister prearrangement, each face wore the same accusing look. My nerves had been on edge so long that I couldn't bear my colleagues' wordless arraignment. Feeling I must get out of the room, I tried to stand up; but, with an elusive sense of recollection, as if I were re-enacting a scene already familiar, I found that I couldn't move. It was the others who rose and silently filed out, leaving me there alone and confused.

Collecting myself with a great effort, I glanced at my watch, for no special reason except that it seemed an every-day commonplace act, and saw that it was midday – they'd merely gone out to lunch as they always did; their departure had no ominous secret significance.

At this moment one of them came in again, walking straight to his desk, which happened to be next to mine. He paid no attention to me but opened a drawer and searched in it, his head bent so that his face was hidden. I knew he was bound to look up in a second; though for the moment I couldn't see his eyes, and the possibility of again meeting accusation in them was intolerable to me, the more so because I'd always liked the look of him better than any of them. His name was Link, and he alone seemed not to share the tough self-interest on which the others prided themselves. He was tall and thin, and his candid blue-eyed face had a look of integrity absent from theirs. I'd always been glad to have him as my neighbour, even though we rarely exchanged a word. Suddenly now I couldn't bear to think that he shared the general suspicion and bad opinion of me and, on the spur of the moment, said, 'I've decided to give up the flat. I shall tell Spector I can't go on occupying two rooms while so many people are homeless.'

He looked at me in surprise. I felt better now I'd declared this sudden intention. I watched him slip some small object into his pocket and then straighten up, growing taller and taller, towering above me, and again an elusive memory was briefly invoked. I forgot about it when he said, 'Spector might not like that', adding quickly, 'Aren't you coming out to lunch?' Obviously, he had found whatever he'd come back for; yet he still seemed in no hurry to go. I told him I would eat a sandwich at my desk as I always did, not mentioning that I didn't like to emphasize my friendlessness by going out alone among the crowds at this time of day; at night, when fewer people were about, I felt less self-conscious. 'That's not enough. You must lunch with me one day soon. I'll show you a good place quite near.' He looked at me a moment longer with a slight frown, as though his good nature were struggling with a different feeling, then turned, and, suddenly in a hurry, went out of the room.

At any other time I'd have been delighted at this sign of relenting. But today I was too distracted and anxious to trust either appearances or my own judgement. Nor could I forget that Link, too, had joined the conspiracy of accusing eyes which had condemned me with such assured unanimity. For all I knew, his return might have been part of some plot they'd all concocted for my further humiliation. Besides, I was troubled by an unaccountable feeling of profound guilt, quite apart from the matter of the flat (which, after all, had been forced on me), as though I were culpable in a deeper sense, which would appal me if I were to face it.

That evening, when I was so depressed I could hardly bear my own company, Spector, by some curious chance, paid me one of his rare visits; it was so long since the last that I'd ceased to expect him. Many times I'd heard steps on the stairs which I'd thought were his, but they'd always stopped lower down, so that I knew they must be those of the night-watchman or of the manager or his assistant, who sometimes worked very late, mysteriously occupied in one of the many storerooms where countless dusty papers were filed away. I didn't even hear the footsteps this time till they were mounting the last flight towards my door, which I hurried to open. Instantly, all my troubles were gone. I still experienced this relief and pleasure whenever I met Spector; in his presence all my apprehensions faded away, as if he supplied a vital quality that I at other times lacked – with him I was no longer vulnerable and exposed; some nameless handicap which usually limited me was removed, so that I could be happy and relaxed at last.

I remember that he was especially charming that evening, taking me out to dine, entertaining me in his usual lavish style. I believe he mentioned some crisis that had kept him from coming to see me before. But I paid little attention to what he said, lost in the sheer luxury of being with him and feeling that words were superfluous because there was between us the constant undercurrent of an understanding far more intimate than speech could ever achieve. Though in my daydreams I liked to play the part of a lonely hero, solitary and proud, to this man I'd relinquished myself utterly; I told myself that I would have rejoiced to show him my inmost secrets, if I'd had any, throwing myself wide open without reserve.

Yet I could see that it was a very one-sided and, in some ways, a very odd sort of relationship. While I wasn't with him, I was aware that it was also an uncomfortable one and possibly even detrimental to me. Though I knew so little about him, the duality which I'd discerned years before made me suspect him of possessing traits I disliked or of which I disapproved; yet I still allowed him to dominate me. I say 'allowed', but, of course, I couldn't prevent it. His power over me was absolute and unchanging; I had only to see him, to come within the radius of his influence, to forget everything else and surrender completely again.

For some time, however, I'd been firmly resolved that at our next encounter this shouldn't happen. I'd made up my mind to discuss certain subjects with him; I wouldn't permit my thoughts to be diverted from them just because he put over me the power of his presence.

For one thing, I was determined to find out his official status at last, not only because it was absurd that I shouldn't know it but also because I'd begun to suspect that he might be connected with the Athing itself – that mysterious hierarchy of anonymous individuals who ruled our lives through the public administrations, of which the Housing Bureau had lately become one of the most important. As I became better acquainted with city life, I'd gradually come to realize how extraordinary and abnormal an atmosphere, evolved out of mass emotion, now surrounded this particular branch of officialdom, an almost metaphysical atmosphere composed of hope, fear and respect, not unlike that which the Church used to enjoy.

Perhaps because I'd been so much alone, having a fairly active brain and little to occupy it, I'd recently been thinking about the collective state of mind, in which people lost all sense of proportion, regarding the possession of a home with superstitious awe and the near-hopeless search for one as a kind of perverted religion, to which they dedicated their time, health, personal relationships, work, peace of mind – everything was demanded by this Moloch before which they cringed, hypnotized by supernatural terrors and impossible hopes. Obviously, a new and most powerful weapon had been put in the hands of the Athing. And I'd been wondering if what appeared like defeatist apathy could be in reality a deliberate policy, an intentional prolongation of all the mental and physical suffering the shortage of houses involved, for the express purpose of fostering this abnormal atmosphere in which officials were exalted to god-head at the public expense – if so, it struck me as cynical and callous in the extreme.

Though I knew it was unwise to jump to conclusions about things I didn't fully understand, I'd developed a highly critical, unsympathetic attitude to the Athing as a whole and the Housing Bureau in particular; I couldn't bear to think of Spector condoning such unprincipled procedures as I suspected. I kept telling myself that I didn't really believe he would; but I must have at least half believed it possible, since I was so anxious to discover the truth. And, as loyalty precluded questioning a third person, the only thing was to ask him directly.

I also wanted to hear his opinion of public events in general and to ask his advice about my private affairs, introducing the delicate subject of leaving the flat. All these were matters of great importance to me; but, though I'd thought about them so long that I knew by heart what I wanted to say, my memory failed me as usual as soon as we came face to face. I quite forgot the questions I'd meant to ask him.

Like a warm tropical sea, his influence surrounded me; far from resisting it, I plunged in gladly, too profoundly submerged even to see the dry land where I existed during his absence. When he congratulated me on my work, of which he'd apparently had good reports, I remember that I didn't realize, though we were in the car, that the evening was already over and that I was being taken back to the flat. It must have been late, for the streets were deserted; with a clear run ahead, the big car travelled fast, developing, in its smooth, uninterrupted rush, a slight swaying motion that made me feel pleasantly drowsy. Dreamily, I sat watching the street lamps flash past, beads of light in an almost continuous chain, while the sculptured profile beside me lightened and darkened, lightened and darkened again.

When we suddenly stopped, I recognized the building with faint surprise. Though the entrance door was on my side, I didn't move but remained in my seat, waiting for my companion to get out first, assuming that he would come in with me, so inconceivable was it to me that I should be parted from him. Some moments passed before began to realize from his immobility that he had no such intention – and even then I couldn't quite believe in the obvious fact but made a protesting sound, before asking in so many words whether he wouldn't come in for a bit, at the same time silently begging him with my eyes not to deprive me yet of the armour of his presence, without which I was at every-one's mercy.

Replying to the words only, he said, quite kindly, that he was very tired and that I must excuse him. Then, as I didn't do it myself, he leaned across me and opened the door; it swung back with a curious sort of finality I couldn't resist, reluctantly getting out to stand on the pavement. I must have still been half dreaming, for I closed the door again and folded my arms on it, looking in at his faintly illuminated face, calm and detached as that of a statue. It was the sight of his indifferent expression that at last really woke me. And now, taking me by surprise, a totally unexpected resentment swept over me, because he was not involved but about to drive off and forget me till he next happened to have nothing better to do than to pay me a visit – and how long would *that* be?

He gave me now a slightly inquiring glance, wondering, doubtless, why I didn't get out of the way. I was evidently more strung up than I realized, swept by a sudden emotion I couldn't control. Before I could stop myself, I'd blurted out the first words to come into my head: 'I don't want to live in your flat any more.' I remember they rather surprised me. I must actually have stamped my foot in impotent infantile rage, for I have an impression of the lifeless jarring hardness of the paving stones. Thus ludicrously expressed, my sudden anger as suddenly ended, leaving me thoroughly dismayed by my own behaviour, foolishly confronting Spector's cool and astonished gaze.

'You need not. I told you at the start you were to live as and where you chose. I merely tried to help you, not to interfere in your affairs.'

His cold voice horrified me. Stammering and incoherent, I began to apologize, leaning into the car, showing my face, in which he could have read all I was unable to put into words: my penitence, my submission, my utter dependence on his goodwill. But he didn't look at me, and his own face remained so cold and stern that I was quite demoralized and would have gone on indefinite with my apologies if he hadn't cut them short.

'The flat's there – take it or leave it. No one else can live in it, anyhow.' Still without turning his head in my direction he said good-night in the same chilly tone. My last glimpse was of his unchanging profile, which might have been hewn out of rock, as my lips shaped an automatic good-night, and I let my arms fall hopelessly at my sides.

I was not very far from tears just then. Whether by association or some other means, he always had the power to reduce me to the emotional status of childhood. And what I felt were a child's sensations: the helplessness, loneliness, inarticulateness; the fear of being forgotten, of not being loved, of being misunderstood – the fear that nobody *ever* would care or would understand.

The great car shot forward abruptly, driving a sudden tremendous blast of air against me, so that I staggered back, the lights swimming dizzily in front of my eyes. And when my vision steadied again, the street was quite empty.

The next day I was deeply depressed, not only on account of this disastrous end to the evening but because I'd told Link so definitely I would leave the flat, and during the night I'd decided, for some obscure reason, that my only hope of reinstating myself with Spector was to stay on there.

Out of a muddled sense of obligation I was always first in the office, as if to start work before the others was the least I could do, since I enjoyed the inestimable privilege of living in the building. On this particular morning, Link happened to come in next, and at the sight of him my loneliness and misery overflowed in a sudden longing for human contact; without stopping to think how odd my confidences would sound to someone I scarcely knew, I impulsively started to tell him, while we had the room to ourselves, why I couldn't give up the flat, though I'd really meant to do so yesterday. He listened patiently while I tried to explain the vital part Spector's goodwill played in my life and how I was afraid of losing it if I left the home with which he'd provided me. It was all simple and self-evident in my mind; but I knew, without looking at my hearer's bewildered face, that I wasn't succeeding in making it clear. Indeed, it seemed quite impossible to convey the peculiar significance of my relations with Spector, of which I'd never spoken to anybody before and which I began to suspect nobody but myself would ever be able to understand. I was relieved when the others came in, interrupting my involved, unintelligible speech.

'I told you he might not like you to leave' was Link's only comment, made with no hint of disapproval or of reproach, while the rest of the staff settled down to the day's work. I looked at him gratefully, pleasantly surprised by his tolerance, and he acknowledged my glance with an understanding smile, which suddenly warmed me, so that some of my depression evaporated and I felt better. My long-winded explanation had achieved something valuable, after all: for the first time since leaving school I seemed to have made a contact with someone.

Later, when Link again proposed lunching together, I gladly accepted, my pleasure only dimmed by the fear of having to give, in greater detail, my reasons for not leaving the flat – I myself hadn't looked into them very closely, instinctively aware that they wouldn't stand careful examination. However, he tactfully kept off the subject – nor did he ever, as far as I can recall, introduce it again. I was more than grateful to him for keeping silent, as by doing so he seemed tacitly to agree with me, exonerating me from blame.

Everyone, I suppose, knows those periods when everything in life seems to conform to a pattern, as though every event and meeting were preordained and carefully timed by a thoughtful providence. Such a period began for me after my unfortunate evening with Spector, from whom I heard nothing more, so that after a while I was forced to conclude I must have alienated him to the point of losing interest in me altogether. For almost my whole life I'd considered the loss of his friendship (if that's the right word) the greatest catastrophe imaginable. Yet now, when the disaster had actually taken place, I suffered far less than I'd expected, events in the outer world all conspiring to soften the blow.

First and foremost, my association with Link provided what was most essential for my distraction: a perfectly normal companion of my own age and one whose special qualities, derived from solid good sense rather than brilliance, were especially useful to me at this time.

A better person couldn't have been found to take me out of myself. And his stability saved me from extremes of emotion, keeping things in perspective and providing me with a sort of ballast out of the steadiness of his own character. Though rather reserved, he was by no means unsociable, and I soon found myself sharing many of his activities. He took me to his home, where his sisters supplied the lightness and gaiety I might have missed in him – the quiet one, as they called him.

I became a frequent visitor there, fascinated by this

introduction to the happy family background I'd never known but for which I'd always felt an unconscious longing. It was so different from anything in my experience that my previous life began to seem like another existence; its happenings grew dim and unimportant, just as the world of imagination faded out like the memory of a dream in the sun, now that I no longer felt in need of an escape from reality.

Either following Link's example or from their own gregarious instincts, the rest of the office staff, seeing me a fixture there, became less hostile. I never made friends with any of them as I did with him, but by slow degrees I found myself absorbed into the collective life of the place; little by little, they came to accept me, though always with reservations.

Gaining self-confidence as my life grew fuller and my circle of acquaintances widened, I thrust the memory of Spector away from me and for long periods scarcely thought about him at all. But, ultimately, a dim regret always recurred. Periodically I would feel sorry that I'd failed to win his affection and that I'd offended him at our last meeting. To forget him entirely was impossible, if only because he sometimes came to the office – though at very long intervals – taking no more notice of me on these occasions than of any other employee.

To see him invariably caused me a faint stirring of uneasiness; a feeling more like guilt than anything, if it has to be classified. I would ask myself then why I'd never made any attempt to bridge the gulf of estrangement that had opened between us – perhaps if I had he would have met me halfway. Considering my indebtedness to him, it seemed no more than my duty to make the effort. But I did nothing, unable to overcome my unwillingness to approach him.

Recalling my childish declaration of loyalty that was to have been eternal, I knew that I was really afraid of coming again under his influence. I dreaded a return to my slavish sub-servience to his will. Yet the idea of going back to him never quite left me; the possibility of a return was always at the back of my mind, though only as a kind of dream-alternative to whatever I happened to be doing, an unspecified 'some-where else', never given a name. Though I felt, on the whole, much happier now that I really seemed to be living the same life as other people, I sometimes had obscure guilt feelings, as if this were not my true destiny and in being dis-loyal to Spector I had also betrayed myself. But, since it was only his actual presence that brought these ideas to the surface, I could afford to ignore them. Most of the time I was proud of my emancipation; my life seemed satisfac-torily full and normal. I was mainly content.

I took to going about a good deal with the elder of Link's sisters, who showed a flattering readiness to cancel other engagements to be my companion. For some time I'd been aware that the family hoped I'd eventually marry and settle down with one of the two, and this girl herself certainly gave me no reason to fear a rebuff if I were to propose. I used to wonder what was restraining me, for the arrangement would have been a happy and appropriate one, establishing me per-manently in the position I wanted to hold – I could never again become an outsider then. It seemed like pure con-trariness on my part to resist this apparently preordained move. Or was I afraid of embarking on a relationship that would invade my inmost privacy? I thought I'd outgrown whatever, during my schooldays, debarred me from close friendship with anyone. But I seem to have been mistaken, judging by a remark Link made, the cause of which I've forgotten, though the words remain in my memory. 'You are a funny chap, Mark,' he said. 'One gets on so well with you; and then you suddenly put up a No Trespassing sign.'

But I might very well have drifted into an engagement in the end, simply because it seemed the obvious thing to do, if I hadn't met Carla, which at once changed my whole life completely.

I'd gone with Link and the girls to dance somewhere. I wasn't much of a dancer, and it was understood that I only functioned in this capacity while no one else was available. When, later that evening, a suitable alternative partner appeared, I was free to leave.

A dance was in progress as I slowly made my way around the room to the door, watching the circling figures intently, searching among them for the one I'd been keenly aware of ever since we arrived, though she was a stranger to all of us. It was the first time in my life I had felt this peculiar interest in someone I didn't know, which made me reluctant to leave without a final glimpse of her.

Link passed, grinning, signalling to me over his partner's shoulder, and, seeing that I was in danger of being reclaimed by our party if I hung about any longer, I went out to the cloakroom. Here a young man I didn't know seemed to be having an altercation with the attendant, but I found my coat for myself and returned to the vestibule, where I at once came face to face with the girl I had been looking for. Oblivious of good manners, I stood staring in a way that would have embarrassed most girls. But she was completely unruffled and cool. Already wearing her coat, she stopped at a mirror beside me and, with almost statuesque composure, began arranging a scarf over her dark hair. I had only to take one long step to reach a position from which I could see her reflection beyond the dim ghost of my own.

It was in the glass that I first perceived a change in the atmosphere, a softer, brighter radiance, reminding me of the setting sun reflected on snow. This limpid brightness I identified with her, as though she were its source; with its delicate glow on her face, she was beautiful and mysterious as a dream; magic was all about her. Spellbound, I ceased to be aware of my surroundings. I no longer had the feeling that I was indoors. That one step I had just taken had carried me over the threshold of magic without transition, as had sometimes happened during my childhood. I was alone with her in some fairy-tale country; a bubble of mirror-magic enclosed us both, outside time and reality.

She hadn't looked at me in the real world; but in the mysterious secret depths of the mirror our eyes met – hers were very large, dark and luminous, almost startlingly brilliant in her clear pale face. She had been from the moment I first saw her immensely, immediately attractive to me; but in ordinary circumstances I would never have dared to stare at her as I was doing now, in the undefined hope of magic coming somehow to my aid – after all, I'd once believed myself a citizen of the enchanted land to which she so clearly belonged. Almost holding my breath I watched her lips part – could she be going to speak to me? Quietly, and as easily as if we'd been old friends, she asked, 'Are you leaving now?'

I suppose I must have said 'Yes', though I was only thinking about her voice, which I found quite enthralling, exceptionally deep for a girl's, with a musical vibrance, in perfect accord with her whole appearance.

Now she turned to ask, in the same natural way, as if we'd known each other for years, in which direction I would be going. But this abrupt transition from magic to reality was too much for me; seeing her, lustrous-eyed and mysterious, no longer mirrored in magic but face to face, I became confused.

It occurred to me, meeting her calm gaze directly, that she'd mistaken me for somebody she knew. Then, with sudden exultance, I realized that she was as aware as I that we'd never met, yet she had made the first move towards me. Magic had overflowed into reality. I felt a quick sort of melting pang, a release of confused feeling; my heart began beating faster. The whole rhythm of my being changed. In astonishment, I supposed this must be falling in love, as, from the midst of the emotional turmoil, I heard my ordinary voice saying firmly, 'I'm going your way.'

In my exalted state it seemed to me that this should have been enough, as though our destiny were already decided, and – to put it crudely – we should be left alone to get on with it, uninterrupted. To my annoyance, however, there was some obstruction. Dimly peering towards this interference, I recognized the young man who had been in the cloakroom; now he hurriedly approached, apologizing for being so long away, and struggling into his coat as he came. He ignored me, only addressing Carla. She was, I observed, more than capable of handling him; she was telling him not to worry, not to break up the party. 'Mark and I are going the same way – we'll go together.'

The sound of my name on her lips gave me a delicious thrill; in her magic ambience it seemed quite natural that she should know it. Passively, I listened to her melodious voice, scarcely hearing the words which dealt so competently with her would-be escort that he was soon accompanying us to the door, smiling and acquiescent. I left the situation entirely to her, as she was so obviously in command of it and only waited impatiently for us to be alone, feeling when we came finally out into the empty street that I had attained something I'd been struggling for all the evening.

Until it happened, nothing could have seemed less likely

than that I should fall in love with a girl I didn't even know and at first sight, too, in this headlong fashion. Nor could it ever have happened, I'm sure, had she not made that initial move which had such great significance for me and set free my blocked emotions. Some obvious integrity she possessed made it impossible to question the impulse on which she had spoken to me; I could only be deeply grateful to her for her courage and quickness in seizing the chance I'd have been too timid and too slow to grasp, prepared in return to give up on the spot the comfortable pattern of life I'd hitherto been determined to preserve.

'There's so little time,' I remember her saying once, apropos of our first meeting. 'And it's all so precarious – senseless. Only pure accident decides whether one meets the right person or passes him in the street; any stranger, almost, might be the one, there's no way of knowing. So if, by some miracle, one *does* know – don't ask me how – isn't it mad not to stop him?'

But this was later. Our conversation that night was devoted to getting to know the ordinary facts about one another, and long before we arrived at her home on the city's outskirts we had ceased to be strangers. She told me she was the only child of rich parents, whose wealth had been devoured by war and taxation, so that, when her father died recently, he'd left little besides this house, in which she and her mother lived – they were even forced to let some of the rooms to make ends meet. I realized that our two worlds weren't the same and had only happened to coincide because of the general chaos of the time. And, as the bus slowly jolted us along, I remember looking out at the maze of unfamiliar streets, contemplating the tremendous odds there must have been against our ever coming together and thinking it really did seem a miracle that we'd met.

And I remember her smiling at me, so that all my tension relaxed, and I smiled back a completely uncensored smile of pure joy; but then, afraid I might have given away too much by showing her my entirely unguarded face, which I never let anyone see, I looked out at the darkness again.

We arranged to meet again next day and were soon meeting daily, for our relationship advanced without a single setback until, after some weeks, with her mother's consent, we became engaged.

Perhaps because I'd never really loved, or entirely trusted, anyone before, it continued to seem miraculous to me to have found a person on whose affection and understanding I could always rely and with whom I could share all my thoughts. That first gesture of Carla's, in throwing a bridge to my isolation, had enabled me to love and be loved, and, gratitude making me all the more dependent, I lived only for her. All my other friends were abandoned without a thought; they just ceased to exist for me. Even Link, who, faithful in his dogged fashion, kept trying to win me back to a more sociable attitude, no longer mattered. Though I was aware of behaving shabbily towards his sister and the family from whom I'd received only kindness, I felt no guilt, for I had no sense of responsibility or obligation except to the girl I loved. With her I was wonderfully happy, living throughout that summer a completely carefree existence. Quite simply, I lost myself in my love and with a luxurious abandonment let everything else go.

An exquisite peace would descend on me as soon as we met, an almost languorous contentment. I'd have liked to stop all the clocks in the world, so that time would stand still. I might have been in a happy trance, and I suppose this was partly why I made no effort to hasten our marriage. But I also felt an instinctive aversion to thinking about the future, as though it were darkened by some obscure foreboding I couldn't even recognize consciously. My rationalization was that I couldn't bear to interrupt our present idyllic companionship; I clung to the carefree serenity of those long summer evenings, which gained a dream-like quality from my knowledge of their impermanence. It was true enough that I dreaded the end of this blissful interlude, which came about so suddenly that I can recall it with extraordinary clarity.

I was in my flat, waiting for Carla at the open window, high above the town. Slanting sunshine was still warm on my face and hands, sunshine still gilded the rooftops and craggy ruins that reached my level, while in the street below dusk was already coagulating, where homebound crowds surged in every direction, like disturbed insects, in seemingly senseless haste. The obvious symbolism of the scene pleased me, the scurrying anonymous people down there in the shadow of darkness, while I was up here in the light. I'd been one of the crowd once, and if I liked I could be one of them again. For the present, I'd withdrawn of my own free will to my gilded tower. For the first time, I felt confident and in control of my life.

But my sense of power was short-lived, vanishing as I realized Carla had raised me up and that, but for her, I should still be priding myself on being just like everyone else. Only a second ago I'd considered the possibility of reverting to what I had been . . . Suddenly I frowned and began to pace the room, unable to avoid the suspicion that I was trying to enjoy both my love affair and my freedom at the same time. This would explain my unwillingness to think of the future and the fact that I never pressed Carla to fix a date for our marriage. Horrible as it was, I couldn't escape the idea that I'd been using my happy entranced state to hide a selfish reluctance to commit myself finally to married life; hating myself for it, I continued to prowl up and down till Carla arrived.

She had barely come into the room, I could barely wait to embrace her, before I begged her to marry me as soon as possible. She looked at me in surprise, smiling at my feverish urgency. Why this sudden tremendous rush? she wanted to know; weren't we quite all right as we were? Her smiling questions, counter-checking my deadly seriousness, suggested a lack of enthusiasm on her part, which at once alarmed me. Perhaps she'd been hurt by my dilatoriness as a lover. Perhaps she was getting tired of me altogether. Increasingly agitated, I implored her still more insistently to decide on a date, finally declaring I'd get a special licence so that we could be married tomorrow.

'And where shall we live? Here?'

Of course, I hadn't overlooked this important point, but I hadn't exactly considered it either, merely assuming that some suitable arrangement could be made without too much difficulty, since we were both the lucky possessors of homes. Now, with an ominous sense of approaching an obstacle I knew had been there all along, my memory began to throw off the oblivion I'd imposed upon it. Against my will and with a sinking heart, I recalled Spector's words – almost the last he had spoken to me – as well as his earlier stipulation. I told myself that neither he nor the authorities could object to my sharing the flat with my wife; yet I was as certain as I'd ever been of anything that, if I were to ask permission for Carla to live here with me after our marriage, it would be refused. How this certainty arose I can't explain; but it was positive enough to make me reply rather hopelessly, 'No, I'm afraid that's quite out of the question.'

Thanks to her, I'd gained confidence. I'd thought myself

independent of the man who was at once my landlord, employer and oldest friend. But that her influence hadn't entirely freed me from his power now became clear, when her puzzled look reminded me of how little I'd told her about him. Of course, I'd often mentioned him and outlined the events in my life in which he'd played a part. Several times I'd been on the verge of describing my relations with him more fully, but, for some unknown reason, I'd always refrained at the last moment. Now I saw I'd be obliged to go into details when she said, 'If he lets *you* live here, why not both of us? Surely, he would, in the circumstances?'

Her beautiful candid eyes were looking straight into mine. Suddenly I was ashamed of my secretiveness, unable to understand why I'd deliberately concealed from her Spector's peculiar hold over me. Taking her hand between both of mine, I told her what he had said; continuing with the whole story, emphasizing his influence on my childhood, the sense I'd once had of being dedicated to him, and my ambivalent attitude towards him that sometimes attracted, sometimes repelled.

In my eagerness to compensate for my earlier secretiveness, I poured out all at once a confusing mass of information that should have emerged bit by bit, at different times, as it fitted naturally into our talk. I complicated it, too, by all sorts of incidents dragged in, regardless of relevance, in the hope of making the picture comprehensive – comprehensible it couldn't have been. It must have sounded like a confession.

I was still holding her hand. I think its inertness was my first indication that I was failing – as I'd failed once before with a different person – to convey the perhaps incommunicable nature of my relationship with this man. But I went on talking, unable to believe she wouldn't suddenly know just what I meant, for she'd always understood me so perfectly.

It was only when lines appeared on her white smooth forehead that I became silent, hating to see her perplexed or troubled. However, they must have been lines of vexation, for she withdrew her hand and, with a certain coldness that matched the gesture, said, 'I'd no idea you were so dominated by Spector. Why didn't you tell me all this before? You ought to see him again and try to make friends.' I wanted to interrupt, to tell her she alone was important to me these days, but, mistaking my intention, she hurried on. 'No, not only because of the flat but because it's obvious that you won't be happy till you're on good terms with him.'

It was our first misunderstanding, the first time I'd heard that chill in her voice, and a sort of desperation made me exclaim, 'I don't care if I never set eyes on the fellow again', continuing more calmly, 'He was only important to me once because I was so lonely. Since I've known you I haven't even thought of him. That's why you haven't heard much about him.' She looked at me gravely without speaking; and I, conscious that I was no longer being strictly truthful, said no more, glad that she didn't pursue the subject.

For the rest of the evening we went on as usual as if Spector hadn't been mentioned. But our gaiety was a trifle forced; I was afraid we'd called up a ghost that wouldn't be easily exorcized. And in that I was right; this was proved afterwards by our mutual inability to speak naturally of the man. Carla rarely uttered his name at all. And, though I refused to revert to my former reserve, I was incapable of talking about him simply and spontaneously; whatever I said seemed to have unintended implications, the most trivial remark developing undertones of startling significance.

The day after our conversation, capitulating deliberately, I admitted there was no real reason I shouldn't ask my employer's permission for the two of us to live here, except that I was already in disfavour and felt certain it would be no good. She answered calmly that I must know what I was talking about – there must be some good reason for thinking he wouldn't help us. Her face was composed and cool-looking, gentle, still, inexpressive. This unchanging composure of hers was sometimes faintly disturbing. It made me wonder now what she was really thinking. But I was glad of it, too, relieved that she didn't want me to approach Spector.

I had, I told her, a much better plan. Why shouldn't we occupy some of the rooms in her home, replacing the present tenants? I'd inherited a little money from my father, and, with this and my salary, I could certainly make up the full amount they were paying, so that her mother wouldn't lose by the arrangement. I smiled, thinking our future already as good as settled, as I put forward this simple and obvious suggestion, wondering why neither of us had thought of it sooner.

To my surprise, Carla shook her head. 'No, I'm afraid that can't be done.' I thought she must be joking, imitating my objections of the previous day, until she went on to explain quite seriously that the rooms were let to officials of the highest grades, who couldn't be asked to leave. 'But, surely, in the circumstances . . .' I began protesting, to break off hastily as I fancied I caught a gleam of amusement in her dark eyes. I seemed fated to make a fool of myself – or was she making a fool of me? Again I was struck by the singularly unrevealing serenity of her expression, her pale, smooth face perfect like a mask, at which I could gaze for ever, it was so clear and lovely. Yet something strange had looked out of her eyes for a moment – strangely disturbing. I'd believed there could never be any misunderstanding between us, but I'd been wrong, and now for a chilling second I seemed not to understand her at all. There was a suggestion about her of something obscure, secret and impenetrable. It was gone almost before I'd seen it; but not before it had brought about a change that proved to be permanent in our emotional climate. It wasn't possible to go back to where we'd been before; nor did I really wish to revert to a stage I seemed suddenly to have outgrown.

Summer was ending. In the sharper, cooler days that ensued, my former languid passivity seemed out of place. Though I loved Carla if possible more than ever, and still experienced in her company hours of relaxed happiness beyond all compare, my contentment now began to develop a reverse side that was correspondingly painful. Uneasy restlessness possessed me all the time we were apart. I was like a nervous traveller waiting for a train, existing in anxiety till our next meeting. If a day passed without seeing her, I became quite distracted, for without her I was lost and incomplete.

With typical spite, life afflicted me with these distressing sensations just when I couldn't possibly be with her as much as before, because I'd started to look for a house for us and saw her only for a short time after the day's search was over and sometimes not even then.

I remember very well how I started searching, diving headlong into the hateful business before my good resolutions had time to cool. This was the day after Carla had said indulgently, 'What a child you are still', stroking my hair while I sat on the floor at her feet. I wouldn't disturb my dream-state to ask what she meant but assumed she referred to my undignified posture, which was one I loved to assume. Resting against her knees, feeling her hand on my head, I was sublimely happy, supremely content. This was all I wanted; just to lean on her, lulled into perfect peace by her rhythmic touch, secure in my dependence, relieved of every responsibility, almost of every thought, existing in a drowsy dream.

Vaguely I contemplated the carpet on which I was sitting,

remotely puzzled because its blurred pattern seemed so very familiar, though I'd never consciously noticed it till this moment, when the dim flowery thickets and tangled scrolls seemed to transfer themselves to the covering of something more resilient than floorboards. Suddenly it was a sofa I was sitting on. The warm protecting body I leaned against was clothed in tweed, through which I could feel the hard muscular masculine flesh, the underlying structure of the male skeleton. My child's face, tingling from outdoor cold, was now beginning to burn in the heat of a fire long since reduced to ash. Yet, at the same time, words just spoken echoed confusingly in my head. Suddenly they ceased to be mere sounds, and I understood them, the floor hardening under me as time moved forward again.

Somewhat bewildered, I thought: But I'm not that child any longer. There was something I certainly shared with the boy so dependent on Mr Spector: thinking of the passive attitude I'd all along adopted towards Carla, as if her original act had fixed our relative positions for all time, it occurred to me that I'd merely exchanged one dependence for another. Perhaps I could only exist under a stronger nature's dominion. But then I insisted to myself that my relationship with Spector had been quite different. There was no comparison; the two couldn't be said to resemble each other in any way.

I jumped up abruptly, pushing a wisp of hair out of my eyes and, seeing Carla sitting there quietly, seized her in my arms. She struggled, laughing, protesting that she couldn't breathe and, when I let her go, looked at me teasingly. 'What's the matter? I believe you were asleep down there – what were you dreaming about?' My only answer was to embrace her again, forgetting my odd little journey into the past, which left me a disquieting legacy, nevertheless. My dependence had suddenly started to make me uncomfortable. I wasn't a child any more. I knew I ought not to hide behind Carla's strength. I ought to go out and grapple with life and find a home for us both. For her sake, I believed I could do anything, even turn myself into a responsible adult person.

This was how I came to start searching for somewhere to live. The prospect of getting involved with the phoney mysticism of the Housing Bureau was so repugnant to me that if I'd had to go far to get there I doubt if my resolve would have stood the strain. But the place happened to be almost next door, down a dreary side street I'd never explored.

Considering its fantastic reputation, and the interdependence of individuals in city life, it was only to be expected that fragments of stories I'd heard should keep coming to me on the way there. I told myself that these tales of frustration and failure had all emanated from people in an abnormal state; no wonder they failed, when they were so agitated, incapable of the thoroughness and perseverance essential to success in any undertaking. It was up to me to avoid their mistakes, to keep cool and above all to make myself impervious to whatever suggestive techniques had induced their semi-hysteria. But wasn't I already falling into the very trap against which I was warning myself, attributing mysterious unknown powers to the Bureau, even before I got there? Thank goodness I still had a sense of the ridiculous. Smiling at my own absurdity, I suddenly felt more confident, very much better. Carla loved me, and that was enough; I needn't fear anyone in the world.

But, all the same, I wasn't exactly looking forward, as I approached the building, to the coming interview with officials who were universally reported to be tyrannical and capricious – though they probably weren't half as bad as they were made out to be, I told myself, and entered boldly.

For a moment I was bewildered by the crowd filling the big room and by the dazzling fluorescent lights, which, presumably, were left on the whole day, for the wire-covered windows must have made the interior dark and gloomy at all times. As I grew accustomed to the scene, the details gradually emerged, and I saw a number of officials seated at large desks, like static islands, around which flowed sluggish streams of applicants, barely seeming to move. Evidently I was in for a long wait. This didn't displease me; it would give me time to form my impressions and to decide which desk to approach.

No one took any notice of me, so I started a tour of inspection, following the narrow irregular spaces between the queues. What first struck me was the uncomplaining patience of all these people, for whom no convenience whatsoever had been provided, not even a wooden bench such as is to be found in the most Spartan waiting-rooms. Yet I observed old people and some who looked ill among them and women with babies in arms. Of course, I blamed the authorities for their lack of consideration; but it seemed to me the public were also to blame for their spineless submission, when, by making a combined protest, they could have got things put right.

After I'd been in the room a few minutes, I found that the light was starting to make my eyes ache. The naked tubes, fixed to the ceiling, diffused a stark white glare which lit up some faces with a ghastly pallor, distorting others by deep black shadows. This dazzle, no doubt, was the reason why all the officials wore eye-shades, extending in front of their faces like the peak of a jockey's cap, casting a black pointed shade, which gave them all a curious similarity to one another, almost as if they were masked.

I could see how a credulous nervous person expecting horrors might find this effect sinister. But to me it was distinctly absurd, as if these dignified figures were sitting at their desks wearing paper caps made out of crackers. I really refused to be overawed by a man in a paper hat; and, humour again coming to my assistance, I decided, since the disguising shadow made it impossible to choose between them, to attach myself to the queue in front of a man who was distinguishable by his fox-red hair from the rest of his anonymous colleagues.

A slight stir diverted my attention, and, like a comment on what I'd been thinking, two hefty attendants in uniform pushed past with a stretcher, on which an old woman was lying unconscious. Her shabby hat, trimmed with a broken feather, must have fallen off and had been planted on her chest beside a worn black bag and some untidy parcels she'd evidently been holding, so that the general effect was of a collection of rubbish being carried off to the dustbin. I was astonished by the indifference of the bystanders, who listlessly drew back to let the stretcher pass, scarcely glancing at its pathetic burden. Their want of interest seemed to show such a fundamental lack of common humanity that, when I noticed a man near by reacting very differently, literally hopping about with rage and scowling at the attendants, I was glad one person at least shared my own feelings, and couldn't resist saying to him, 'Isn't it outrageous? Why don't people complain?'

At the sound of my voice, he turned and glared at *me*, perched on one leg, clutching the other foot with both hands, so that I belatedly realized he was angry because his toe had been stepped on, not on the old woman's account, as I'd imagined. 'Who are you? What's your game?' he muttered with such venom that I was thankful a sudden forward movement of the crowd separated us, taking him out of my sight. And soon after this it was my turn to stand in front of the official's desk.

He, seeing I was the last person he'd have to deal with, had already begun to relax, leaning back, pushing his eyeshade up at a rakish angle and rubbing his eyes, revealing an unexpectedly young lively face. 'Last but not least, eh?' he said cheerfully, rather as if enjoying a secret joke in which I was involved.

Nothing could have surprised me more than his behaviour and appearance, and I probably showed this, for he seemed to become more amused, while continuing to rub his eyes, exclaiming, 'Lord, what a day! The weekends are always the worst, but today's been a record.'

I was tempted to reply that he wasn't the one to complain; and, as if to some extent reading my thoughts, he went on, 'I suppose you think mine's an easy job. But I can tell you it's abominably tiring, sitting here all day under these infernal lights – you must have noticed how hard they are on the eyes – being badgered by everyone. We do our best to help people. It's not our fault the accommodation just isn't available. We'd be only too pleased to bring houses out of our pockets like conjurors if we could. That's what people seem to expect, always blaming us if they're disappointed, when they ought to blame our superiors.'

Having braced myself to confront a sadistic tyrant, it was disconcerting, to say the least, to be faced with this ordinary, rather pleasant, harassed-seeming young man, who appeared anxious for my good opinion. But, remembering the old woman who'd been carried out, I said severely, 'If you're really doing your best, there's no need to defend yourself.' Rather alarmed by my boldness, I hesitated; then, as he said nothing, went on, 'I can't say anything, because all I know about the place is what I've been able to observe in the last half-hour – which certainly hasn't impressed me very favourably.'

'There! You see, it's just as I said; we get the blame for everything. Of course, it's very convenient for the people above us . . .' Breaking off, he pulled some forms towards him and asked in a different tone, 'And now, what can I do for you?' But he seemed unable to forget his private joke, for, leaning forward so suddenly that the eye-shade slipped on one side, dangling drunkenly over his ear, he planted his elbows on the desk and stared at me with an inquisitive, keen, amused look. 'You're one person I did *not* expect to see here, I must say. You surely don't want to move out of a flat anyone else would give his ears for?'

'What? Do you know who I am, then?' I exclaimed, taken aback.

'Good Lord, yes. We know all your family history here. In fact, you're quite a celebrity among us.'

Though he was clearly enjoying the surprise he had just sprung on me, his expression wasn't unfriendly. In fact, his wide mouth stretched into a grin so disarming that it reassured me. Regaining confidence, I told myself that anyone might have used the words 'family history' and that they had no sinister personal meaning: my case was bound to be known to the whole Housing Bureau, being unique of its kind.

Looking at the red-haired man, I felt I'd reached the crucial point where I had to decide whether or not I was going to trust him – and really I saw no valid reason not to, dismissing a vague suspicion that he might have been told to extract information from me; for what information could he extract, beyond what was already known? I had no guilty secrets, I'd done nothing to be ashamed of. On the contrary,

I was extremely proud of my fiancée, so why shouldn't I tell him about her? He seemed genuinely well disposed towards me and might be willing to help us. So, having argued myself out of my initial slight distrust, I briefly explained the position, though without reference to Spector's stipulation. Feeling my usual reluctance to speak about him, I merely stated that there were private reasons why I couldn't live in the flat as a married man. Would he help me and give me the benefit of his advice?

He seemed to reflect for a moment, tapping his fingers on the top of the desk as if playing the piano; then, perhaps gratified by my request, to which I'd tried to impart a flattering sound, he replied genially, 'One tip I can give you of a practical nature, and that is to come in the evening. We only see applicants once a day, and nearly all of them come in the early morning, on their way to work. You should see the queues outside the doors then – we literally have to fight our way in some days. Today's Saturday and an exception; in the ordinary way you'd hardly find a soul here at this time. I advise you to slip round after you finish work; you'll just do it if you hurry, being so near, though other people haven't got time – that's where you'll score over them. The morning's accommodation will have been allocated long before, naturally, but you'll automatically be first on the list for whatever may have come in during the day.'

I thanked him gratefully, for, in spite of my inexperience, I could see that his suggestion was of real value; and when he started taking down my requirements I tried to repay him by supplying the details with a conciseness born of familiarity with office routine. His appreciation was evident when he said at the end, 'If only the others were more like you, we'd get through in half the time.'

I was feeling very pleased with the luck of my haphazard

choice, which had led me to this friendly, communicative person, from whom I was finding out things, instead of the other way around. Perhaps I'd be able to elicit some more information by judicious questioning: in this hope I now held out the elegant silver cigarette case Spector had given me. He admired it, saying, 'I can guess where that came from', and gave me a confidential glance I didn't quite like, though I realized how unfair it was to associate a foxy slyness with his red hair. Returning the case to my pocket, I was about to produce a light when he stopped me by making a low negative sound and shaking his head.

I looked up to see a girl in a white blouse and black skirt approaching us. The big room was now almost empty of applicants, and a number of these girls – secretaries, I presumed – had appeared while I wasn't looking and were everywhere darting towards the desks already vacated, rapidly putting in order the jumble of papers left behind there and carrying off the outgoing letters. Those of them who had to wait to get at a desk where work was still going on did so with undisguised impatience, like the one hovering around us, who was coming closer and closer, making a good deal of noise with her feet. Her restless fidgeting obviously irritated my red-haired acquaintance, and I expected him to reprimand her; instead, he suddenly jumped up and, signing to me to follow, strode across the room, the eye-shade detaching itself, floating behind him with a glider's motion, till the girl pounced on it indignantly.

I assumed that smoking must be forbidden. But his only object apparently was to escape her, for, as soon as we were out of earshot, he stopped and lit both our cigarettes. 'It's an anachronism, employing those wretched girls,' he remarked. 'But I suppose they're cheaper than tape recorders and fulfil the same function.'

Not quite understanding him, I merely asked why he hadn't sent her away. But he answered evasively, as if distracted, and, as there seemed to be nothing more to be got out of him then, I said goodbye, reflecting on my way out that his powers couldn't be very great if he wasn't able to control an impertinent secretary.

On the whole, though, I was very satisfied with the result of the interview and hurried back to tell Carla about it.

Even if Ginger (as I called him, since he hadn't told me his name) wasn't in a position to order the secretaries about, he must have considerable influence with his superiors, as he and his colleagues formed their only link with the public. Putting out of my mind the disturbing memory of the old woman, I'd convinced myself that there was nothing sinister about the Bureau. And, just as the officials had turned out to be quite human, so, I was sure, the whole business of finding a home would prove far less formidable than I'd been led to believe. I was young and optimistic, and I thought I had made an excellent start and would soon win through to the success so many better-qualified people had failed to achieve.

Throughout our brisk invigorating autumn my confidence inspired me to continuous effort. I was all the time encouraged by Ginger, whose advice I valued even more highly when I discovered how many applicants had been attending the Bureau for long periods without ever getting a chance to look at a house, whereas I nearly always received the addresses of a few properties, which I invariably set out to inspect with high hopes, notwithstanding the fact that somebody else always snapped them up before me, if they weren't hopelessly dilapidated or far too expensive. My hopes seemed to flourish on disappointment in those days, renewed again and again each time I assured myself that if not this house then certainly the next would be the very place I was looking for.

The only thing that worried me was that I saw so little of Carla, who, though she waited patiently at the flat for my return, had to leave at eleven to catch the last bus back to her home. More and more often as autumn merged into winter and bad weather increased the difficulties of getting about, I came back so late that we could spend only a few minutes together. Though she assured me she didn't mind, it distressed me to think of her wasting her evenings like this. I vaguely supposed I ought to urge her to stay at home instead of coming so far, in such miserable circumstances, for the sake of so short a meeting. Yet I never tried seriously to prevent her from coming. The fact was, I felt I couldn't have carried on at all without these brief encounters, which enabled me to keep under control the anxiety that now always tormented me while we were apart.

This anxiety was all the time growing stronger, in the longer and longer periods of separation from her, when she seemed incredible to me, as if I had dreamed her, and I struggled vainly to recall her real face. Her mysterious aspect appeared more and more frequently in my thoughts. I saw her as some lovely, tall princess, with her white skin made whiter by contrast with her lustrous dark hair and darkly shining eyes; and this was all I could see. It was as if I'd never seen how she looked in real life but only overlaid by the strangeness, the unattainable otherness, of her dream counterpart. Whenever we were together I would keep gazing at her, trying to learn her real face like a lesson, in which I many times thought I'd become perfect. But afterwards she again wouldn't seem true; mystery would once more obscure her. Only the strangeness seemed real, the reality as elusive as ever. Every time we parted I was afraid it was the end, that she was lost to me and would never come back.

My rational self wouldn't acknowledge these childish fears or tried not to. But as time went on they grew more powerful and, refusing to stay in the background, forced themselves into my consciousness. Then I could only exist for the moment when I'd catch sight of her and prove them false. Day by day, tension was increasing, anxiety gradually infiltrating everywhere but so insidiously I hardly noticed the process till it was complete, and I woke one morning to a different world, as if, while I slept, a giant's hand had jolted everything into a new and hateful perspective.

It now seemed to me that there was a worldwide conspiracy among people and things to keep me from Carla. Every day, all day, I was contending with people, stupid or obstructive or malicious or inefficient, impeding and delaying me. And with frustrating things: trains and buses that slid away as I pursued them; streets leading me astray or becoming impassable dead ends; fogs blinding me; gales snatching vital papers out of my hands; the frequent sluicing punishment of sleet and rain. And always, worse than any of these, the conspiracy of the seconds and minutes to group themselves into hours – hours I should have been spending with Carla – until the agonizing climax of uncertainty when I began to doubt whether I'd get back in time to see her at all.

Gradually, I was losing heart, discouraged by my repeated failures. And now anxiety began to invade even the precious hours when we *were* together. I couldn't entirely suppress the thought of her waiting for me so long alone; and perhaps an unconscious hope of expiation increased the despondency her presence could no longer charm away as in the past. Though I was ashamed of myself, I started being sulky and difficult with her. She was always the same, calm and sweet-tempered, apparently unaware of my bad behaviour, which she took with a smile of detached good nature that only made me want to break out in fresh excesses, to say rude, hurtful, unforgivable things. Yet I absolutely adored her; she was hardly ever out of my thoughts; night and day I longed for her with a passionate tenderness. I can't explain now, any more than at the time I could understand, why as soon as we came face to face there seemed only her dark romantic beauty, as if her real self eluded me.

Finding myself, as it were, in love with a lovely dream, I was slowly becoming resentful and discontented. I felt cheated, angry, aggrieved. The familiar bitter grievance I'd felt for so long because people and things were opposed to me gradually added itself to these other resentments, extending finally to include Carla herself, leading up to the shocking revelation that she had become a part of the universal hostility I was fighting. I was, I remember, giving my usual account of the houses I'd just seen, when, looking at her serene, composed face, I suddenly felt her strength, on which I had always depended, turned into an alien driving force, compelling me to continue this unprofitable search.

Instead of going on with my objective report, I began to complain resentfully of all the frustrations, discomforts and difficulties I'd suffered during the day; and after this fell more and more frequently into the habit of querulousness, voicing my complaints as bitterly as though she were directly to blame for all I had endured. My resentment seemed to rise from somewhere deep down in me, from some spring of which I knew nothing; and I thus made the disturbing discovery of some obscure process going on in me that I could neither understand nor control.

I'd always regarded as pure superstition the notion that

the Bureau exerted an evil influence over those who had dealings with it. But that *something* was causing me to deteriorate I was forced to admit, feeling my will, integrity, independence gradually undermined, till it seemed as if the very structure of my being was threatened with ultimate collapse. The strange and frightening thing was that I made no attempt to arrest this destructive process, which, though alarming, actually had a kind of morbid fascination for me.

Nothing could keep me away from the Housing Bureau these days. Though Carla and I had originally decided always to keep the weekends free for one another, I'd lately taken to visiting the place on Saturdays and Sundays as well as during the week, drawn there by this inexplicable attraction that had nothing to do with my longing to find a home. When Christmas approached, I was actually depressed by the prospect of the Bureau being closed for several days, a circumstance my normal self would have welcomed.

I wasn't much looking forward to Christmas in any case, as Carla's mother insisted on keeping her at home to help with the extra work entailed by the festivities. I'd agreed to share their dinner on Christmas Day, in spite of having received – how I hardly know – an impression somewhat less than friendly from my prospective mother-in-law on the few occasions we'd met. When the time arrived, on top of everything else, I had a bad cold, caught, I suppose, in the course of my uncomfortable travels. I didn't feel like going anywhere or doing anything and willingly promised Carla to spend Christmas Eve indoors.

However, during the afternoon I became restless, wandering from one room to the other and wondering whether, in view of the days which were to elapse before the Bureau reopened, I might not be missing a chance by not going there now. In the end, I seized my coat and hurried down the stairs. I must have meant to go all along.

Outside it was freezing hard, the streets were bleak and deserted, in contrast to the lighted trees standing gaily in many windows. I could see rooms decorated with evergreens and family parties assembled, as though everyone were at home, and told myself that for once the Bureau would be empty.

Instead, I saw, as soon as I entered, that it was exceptionally crowded. The flaring lights and the heat generated by so many tightly packed bodies made me feel dazed at first. I couldn't see Ginger's desk and started pushing my way through the people, who seemed to obstruct me deliberately, pressing so closely about me that I was very soon brought to a standstill. A heavy hand fell on my arm, and I realized that I'd been stopped by one of the attendants, who usually did nothing more active than stand about reading the newspapers, except when required to act as stretcher-bearers. Ordering the man to release me, I asked indignantly since when it had been part of his duty to keep applicants away from the officials. He seemed a bully of the worst type, for he only gripped me tighter and said roughly, 'I saw what you were up to, shoving people about and creating a disturbance; and so did all these . . .' jerking his head to indicate the circle of people, whose faces, corpse-like under the lights, ringed us around.

Now I noticed with surprise how they, usually so indifferent to what went on, were staring at us with evident interest. Many of them, eager to curry favour, nodded or made sounds of assent. I was disgusted by their readiness to bear false witness against me and to agree with any preposterous statement. It made me furious, too, to feel the attendant's dirty fingers nipping my arm all the time; but I knew I was unequal to a tussle with him and instead directed my indignation again the bystanders.

'Why do you take sides with this fellow?' I asked angrily. 'Don't you see you're only making things worse for yourselves? He's supposed to be a public servant. You, the people who pay his wages, do you pay to be bullied? It would be better if you got together and lodged a complaint against *him*.' No one answered me. Nobody said a word. The circle of white faces, distorted by black shadows, had the look of identical white paper masks, ghoulish, grotesque and unreal. In a final attempt to rouse them to some response, I went on, 'Look at the way this place is run – it's a perfect scandal. The high authorities show not the slightest consideration for the people they're supposed to be helping. But if everyone complained, something would have to be done in the way of improvement.'

There was dead silence when I finished speaking. The usual drone of voices at the various desks had ceased. To my amazement, I saw that I really did seem to have disrupted the normal routine. People had everywhere broken their ranks and were craning towards me, leaning on one another's shoulders to see me better; livid, shadow-slashed faces, all with the weird family likeness the lighting gave, were everywhere staring at me. But now that I'd gained this universal attention, my indignation deserted me. My head felt hot and heavy; the mass of identical, undifferentiated faces bewildered me. Suddenly it struck me that my own face must look just the same as theirs, and for some reason this was both depressing and profoundly distasteful to me. I let my head droop as if to conceal my resemblance to all these people. I had the feeling I was letting them down. But all I could do was wait passively for the attendant to release me, which he showed no sign of doing, glancing about all the time as if expecting the arrival of a superior who would give him his orders. Such a person, in fact, was now approaching. A head could be seen, shining fierily under the lights above the disguising eye-shade which hid the face I knew must be Ginger's, even when he came close enough to whisper to the man holding me, who at last, with extreme promptness, let me go.

I was struck by the way the onlookers, losing all interest in me, turned back, like so many clockwork figures, to their respective queues as throughout the room the usual sluggish procedure went on again, as if it had never been, could never be, interrupted. For a moment this distracted me. By the time I'd realized I should have been thanking Ginger for his intervention, he was already hurrying back to his desk. I had to follow him through the crowd, pursuing him with my thanks under difficulties, unable to tell whether or not he was listening to what I said. Since he ignored me, I took my place at the end of the queue in front of his desk, automatically rubbing my arm, still sore from the attendant's grasp.

When I arrived before him, I was astonished by the hostility with which I was greeted. 'There's never anything for you at weekends. Why can't you keep away instead of coming here making trouble?'

He sounded so irritable that I hastily answered him, 'I didn't mean to make trouble for *you*. I only said people ought to complain to the higher authorities, and you told me yourself –'

'We're the ones who'll have to suffer for it,' he interrupted tartly, at the same time beginning to collect various objects from his desk and standing up, preparatory to departure.

'Please don't go yet!' I exclaimed quickly, making a futile attempt to intercept him. 'You surely can't believe I'd be so ungrateful –' But he was determined not to give me a hearing and walked off without even saying goodbye.

There was nothing left for me to do but go back to my flat, which I did, very much perplexed by the sudden change in someone who, up to now, had always been affable and obliging. His bad temper struck me as unreasonable. And it was certainly most unfortunate in view of the time that would have to elapse before I saw him again, as he was bound to retain an unfavourable impression of me till after the holiday, when it might be too late to eradicate it. There were other aspects of the incident that I found incomprehensible and disturbing. If he'd really believed I was inciting people against him, why had he come to my rescue? And what could he possibly have said to the attendant to make him drop my arm like a hot potato?

It was partly to rid my mind of these unanswerable questions, which continued to worry me the next day, that I set off for Carla's home in the early afternoon, arriving at the bus terminus before the short winter daylight had come to an end. All my previous visits had been in the evening; I'd got only a vague impression of large houses standing in their own gardens. Now I was delighted by the openness of the scene, to which many tall trees gave an almost rural look. I felt as if I'd arrived in the country, and my pleasure made me realize how much I'd missed the wide landscape, the hills and valleys and woods which had always been my background before I came to the city, and how unsuccessful I'd been in making myself feel at home here.

Stimulated by the frosty, clear air and the glow of the setting sun upon snow-covered lawns and lanes, I decided to explore a little before going indoors, as Carla wouldn't be expecting me yet. I forgot all about my cold as I hurried up a steep hill, hoping to reach a point where the houses gave way to open country before darkness fell. In this I was disappointed: I only managed to lose myself and hadn't the faintest idea where I was when twilight deepened into dark. This was really awkward, as there wasn't a soul about of whom I could inquire. I thought of asking at one of the houses, but they all stood far back from the road, the street lamps were few and far between, I could scarcely see the black roofs looming against the sky; and, far too tired to walk up one of the long drives, I kept on blindly, in a kind of blank stupor of weariness, arriving finally at Carla's house completely worn out and in anything but the mood for a party.

She opened the door herself and must have noticed how exhausted I was, for she asked whether I'd like to rest in the library for a bit before meeting her mother and the official who was also to be their guest – the only one of the tenants to stay over the holiday. This I was very glad to do, grateful for the chance to recover in private, and, as soon as I was alone, stretched out on a sofa. But I could only relax for a few minutes, after which my usual anxiety again claimed me. The sofa was hard and the room too cold for comfort. Unable to hear a sound from the rest of the house, I soon started feeling aggrieved and neglected and wondering why I was left alone there so long. At the end of an interminable half-hour I got up and began to prowl around the room, keenly aware of Carla's heartlessness in abandoning me, with my bad cold, in this freezing room. All of a sudden it became impossible to stay there any longer. I went out into the passage, somehow found my way through the strange house without encountering anyone, and arrived finally in the entrance hall where, ages ago as it seemed, I had hung my coat.

I don't know what childish impulse made me hide behind it now when I caught sight of her through the open door of the dining-room, looking lovelier than I'd ever seen her in a dress of some silvery stuff, from which her bare arms and shoulders rose like a naiad's from some moon-bright cascade. As if mesmerized by her cool beauty, I stood staring while she put the finishing touches to the table, where tall candelabra shed their calm light on a profusion of fruit and flowers, sparkling glass and silver and gem-like ornaments. This dazzling display of luxury contrasted most strangely with the cold desolate room I'd just left, renewing my sense of grievance. I was wondering how on earth she and her mother could afford such lavishness, when, as if in answer to my unspoken question, a third person appeared, crossed the hall without turning towards me and entered the dining-room with the confident step of a man on his own home ground.

I knew this must be the official I'd never met, a total stranger to me, of whose face I hadn't caught a glimpse, whose name even was unknown to me. All I could see of him was his back, as he stood beside Carla; yet there seemed something familiar about that massive outline – so much so that I felt I'd have recognized him if he'd turned around. Occupied with this odd impression, I missed what he said and saw only Carla's responsive glance of intimacy; the brilliant breathtaking loveliness of her face caused me a sharp pang as she lifted it to him, for I'd believed that uncovered beauty and intimate smile belonged to me alone. It was almost as cold in the hall as it had been in the library, yet I felt a curious hot shock of anger, as if I'd been robbed by this stranger, whose dark silhouette produced the effect of being slightly larger than life, as he now leaned towards her with a solicitude that confounded me still further by suggesting a deeper familiarity, as of figures not quite remembered but seen in the same pose long ago.

The mists of childhood beginning to thicken around me, I reluctantly groped my way back among ghosts and half memories. To the sharp pain and angry shock, the man had added something heavily ominous that belonged to the past; he himself seemed the core of some old dream that was almost nightmare – from which, I suddenly realized, it was necessary for me to escape immediately at all costs. Without a word, without another glance in the direction of the dining-room, I took my coat and fled.

At first, stumbling away from the big house in the icy dark, my only thought was to remove myself as quickly as possible and as far from the place where imperfectly recognized ghosts had confused and tormented me. Then, recovering quickly once I was alone, I got my bearings from the lights of the bus terminal. Luckily a bus was on the point of leaving, and, sitting among the empty seats, being carried towards my flat, I felt my normal equilibrium return.

Why had I rushed away like that? What had happened? I asked myself, with an uneasy feeling that I'd acted foolishly. Nothing, apparently, had happened except in my head, where momentarily that larger-than-life form again loomed up, the personification of some inescapable threat at the heart of an old dream I couldn't entirely forget but refused to remember, concentrating instead on the real incident.

My memory of recent events was quite clear, even though obscure dream-like notions still haunted the back of my mind. Ignoring these, I saw how badly I had behaved, and the instant I got home telephoned to apologize, telling Carla my cold had suddenly got much worse, which seemed the only possible justification for my abrupt disappearance. Yet, even while I was speaking humbly to her, genuinely contrite, I was aware of a grievance, a vague suspicion; I couldn't help feeling she'd treated me badly, though she'd always before been so considerate. Listening to her low musical voice, in which I could detect no personal warmth, I began to feel immensely removed from her; a million miles of darkness divided us.

But then I was suddenly projected into a quite different magic world, where depression, grievance and distrust couldn't exist. I'd expected to be alone the next evening; now Carla proposed spending it with me, her mother having received a last-minute invitation, so that she herself would be free. This seemed to prove my importance to her, and immediately everything came all right again. Only in my jealous imagination had she smiled at a stranger with the intimacy she reserved for me. The prospect of her visit was like a wonderful surprise present; in the delight and excitement of its reception I expected perfection in every detail, my cold was to cure itself automatically during the night. I felt disappointed and cross when it seemed rather worse in the morning.

At any rate, I thought, there would be no temptation today to go out, since the Housing Bureau was closed. But as the afternoon dragged on, restless anxiety once more afflicted me. The sombre cloud-roof, which had all day covered the sky, towards three o'clock became in the west faintly burnished, soon afterwards extinguishing the last of the daylight. By four it was as dark as midnight.

Still three more hours had to pass before I could even begin to expect Carla. How would I ever get through three whole hours? My impatient longing for her was insistent, distracting; far worse than the dull pain behind my forehead. I was aware, too, of another unanalysed feeling, sinister and heavy and uncomprehended, fixed at the root of my anxiety, which I would not examine. I couldn't stand it and, suddenly jumping up, went out of the flat and down the stairs; I simply had to go out – to do something.

The air out of doors, though bitingly cold, seemed somehow oppressive; some blocked electrical tension, struggling to find an outlet, exerted its pressure upon my nerves as I tramped along heavily under my aching head, not thinking of where I was going.

Seeing lighted trees in the windows and wreaths on the doors, family parties assembled in decorated rooms, I seemed to have gone back to Christmas Eve. Everything was repeating itself: the empty streets and these unreal celebrations behind the glass, which might have been taking place on another planet for all the contact I could ever conceivably have with them. It didn't surprise me to find myself in front of the Housing Bureau. Where else could I have arrived?

But then I saw the place closed and dark, a metal grille barricading the entrance. Of course. The Christmas holiday; how could I have forgotten? I felt a passing uneasiness, troubled by my unnatural-minded vagueness. Deciding to put it down to my headache, I promptly forgot all about it, advancing, for no particular reason, towards the protective bars and running my hands over the cold steel. If I hadn't done this I would never have discovered the existence of an unobtrusive opening about the size and shape of a man; a wicket at which I gazed for a while in perplexity, wondering why it had been left open and whether I ought to shut it.

Having made up my dull mind it was no business of mine, I was about to start walking home when, in the street I'd thought absolutely deserted, a passer-by stopped to stare at me with a persistent disapproving inquisitiveness that could only mean that he regarded me as a suspicious character loitering there. My reactions were not normal just then. It didn't occur to me that, had I drawn his attention to the open gate and told him what was in my mind, his suspicions would have been removed and he would most likely have proved quite friendly. Instead, for some reason, I felt obliged to remain silent and motionless as long as he was watching me. He walked on, constantly turning his head to look back at me as long as I was in sight, reluctant to leave me to my evil devices. And only when he at last disappeared did I feel free to go home. Then, turning in that direction, I saw a whole group of people coming towards me whom I'd been too preoccupied to notice before, presumably from some local gathering that had just broken up.

As I've said, I was not in a normal state and can only suppose some degree of fever accounted for my behaviour now. I had done nothing wrong. Nor had I anything to fear from these new arrivals, doubtless law-abiding citizens like myself, who so far hadn't observed me. There was no real reason for the intense anxiety to avoid their curious eyes that made me slip through the aperture into the shadows beyond the grille and flatten my body against one of the massive entrance doors as they passed.

Evidently I had succeeded in making myself invisible, for no inquisitive glance came my way. The last stragglers of the party had just gone by; another second and I'd have stepped outside the metal network again. But before I had time to move, while I was still leaning all my weight on the door, this support gave way behind me with such unexpected suddenness that I fell back with it. My arm was seized in a bewilderingly familiar grasp, I was dragged back still further, and the door shut again, in front of me this time, shutting me into what seemed total darkness.

In my already confused state I now became – for a space of time almost too brief to record – panic-stricken, my captor's hateful touch evoking a whole chain of agonizing sensations. I ceased to be myself, feeling my being invaded by the personality of a criminal; the hand on my arm was the grip of the law – of the police, by whom I'd been arrested. What crime I'd committed I didn't know; nor did this matter, since I knew I was guilty, and guilt itself was my crime. The shades of the prison house already enclosed me. There was no hope. I was being dragged deeper into some weird cavernous darkness, lit only by glow-worm glimmers of greenish light. Never again, I thought despairingly, should I see the sun.

That all these impressions occupied only the merest fraction of time was proved by the fact that I hadn't even regained my balance when someone exclaimed, 'Hold up, there!' continuing, as I steadied myself, 'Sorry, but I had to make sure nobody saw you come in, or we'd have had the whole population battering on the doors.' The matter-of-fact, disembodied voice helped me to return to myself and to expel the intruder who had burdened me with his crime, as it concluded, 'There's news for you. Come this way.'

I'd already collected myself sufficiently to recognize the big room, which I'd previously always seen crowded and brightly lit, now dark and empty, only a few heavily green-shaded desk lamps scattered about. Though I wasn't agitated any longer, I still felt half dazed by the shock of what had seemed my abduction and the associations it had aroused. I was so relieved now because the hand on my arm seemed kept there to guide and support, rather than to take me into custody, that I allowed myself to be led further into the darkness. I had no idea who was escorting me; there wasn't nearly enough light to identify faces or even the colour of hair. The voice hadn't sounded like Ginger's, though, on the other hand, it was too cultivated to belong to one of the attendants. These reflections, too, helped restore my normality, while simultaneously arousing an undefined suspicion, which, despite its vagueness, at this point made me stand still and ask, 'Where are you taking me?'

'To the chief's private office.' Besides sounding surprised by my question, the speaker seemed to consider me unappreciative, for his tone became definitely reproachful. 'He's been waiting for you all the afternoon, though I happen to know he was looking forward to being at home for his children's party today. "Go and look out for him," he told me when it got dark. "I particularly want him to have the news today since it wasn't possible to let him have it in time for Christmas."' Thinking, no doubt, that he'd put me to shame by relating this instance of official benevolence, he again urged me on.

But now I'd once more got my wits about me and refused to move. 'How could he possibly have known I would come at all?' I asked sharply, gratified by the firmness of my voice and the sensible sound of the question, which received no reply beyond a repeated request to hurry up that I ignored.

My suspicions were all the time growing stronger and more defined. I'd become completely sceptical about the 'news', which I was sure would turn out to be some sort of fraud. We happened to be standing close to a desk, on the top of which the lamp cast a greenish circular glow like that of a night light. In the deep shadow beyond it I seemed to discern the dim shape of a seated figure, leaning forward a little, in an attitude of intense watchfulness. As if this provided the clue to the whole situation, my suspicions suddenly crystallized into certainties. All at once, everything seemed to stand out in a burst of illumination.

Recalling how the red-haired man had taken offence and

gone off without speaking to me, I felt convinced, in my new enlightenment, that everything that had taken place here today was part of an elaborate hoax, of which I was to be the victim. Fortunately, I'd seen through it. But I shuddered to think of the shock and disillusionment a more trusting person would have been in for and felt an obligation to protest, however ineffectively, against this heartless trick. 'A cruel joke,' I said coldly, putting as much sternness into my voice as I could.

'Joke?' my companion echoed, taken aback, presumably, because I'd already discovered the plot – or could it be that he knew nothing about it? His surprise sounded so genuine that the possibility of his innocence crossed my mind but seemed too wildly improbable to consider seriously, so I said, as coldly as before, 'Tell your friend the chief, or whatever he calls himself, to choose another sucker next time. I'm not so easily fooled.'

With this, I disengaged myself from the unresisting hand on my arm and began groping my way back to the door by which I'd entered so unceremoniously. To my surprise, no attempt was made to detain me. If each light represented a hidden watcher, there must have been a good many of them in the room; they could easily have overpowered me between them. But, like the bullying petty tyrants they were, they seemed to have collapsed completely as soon as I stood up to them. Throughout the great echoing place nobody moved; there wasn't a sound, apart from the noise of my own blundering progress.

Growing bold, I went up to one of the desks I was passing, meaning to look into the face of the shadowy form sitting there, apparently watching me. But either the greenish light was distorting or I was still in a confused state, for I got the somehow dismaying impression that I was confronting a mere bundle of clothing propped up in the chair, instead of a human being and stumbled away, disconcerted, without further investigations.

I'd found the door at last and was on the point of opening it when the individual to whom I'd been speaking overtook me and held out a paper, saying, 'Since you won't come to the chief, he sends you this.' My hand clenched automatically to crumple it in disgust; but then I hesitated, hearing, 'A room has just become vacant in the street where your fiancée lives, and he thought you might like to take it until you find somewhere suitable for you both.'

So Ginger insisted on playing his pitiless farce to the bitter end. How well the messenger was acting his part; that simple sincere voice and manner of his didn't match the idea of deception. Though I knew the thing must be a fake, I couldn't entirely suppress the thrill of pleasure that stirred my nerves at the prospect of living near Carla. I found that I was wavering, undecided. *Could* I trust this messenger with the convincing voice? On a sudden impulse, determined to get a glimpse of his face, I abruptly opened the door, admitting a wedge of pale light from outside. There, straight in front of me, was the narrow exit, at which I gazed with such relief that I might have been afraid it wouldn't be there any longer. But it was the messenger who, in the brief moment while I was looking at it, seemed to have vanished. Peering into the dimness, I saw no sign of him anywhere, till a slight stir in the dense black shadow behind the door suggested that he'd concealed himself there when I opened it.

'So you're afraid to let me see your face!' I exclaimed indignantly. 'I'm not surprised, after trying to play me such a mean trick with that sham document.' I held the paper out in the light, hoping he would come forward to take it, so that I'd be able to see him. He didn't move, and I went on in disgust, 'You're just as bad as the others. Heaven only knows why I should have imagined you might have retained some vestige of decent feeling. I see what a fool I've been to trust any of you, to believe you were trying to be helpful. You officials must have been laughing your heads off all this time. Well, my eyes are open at last. Now I can see you all in your true colours – corrupt, irresponsible, deceitful and totally callous. Not one of you cares a damn for the people you're supposed to be helping. No wonder you're ashamed to show yourselves when you indulge your infantile sadism at their expense in this sort of spiteful play-acting!'

Silence closed on my angry voice, and I knew my anger was partly assumed. Was anyone listening to me? I could no longer be certain of the dark shape I thought I had seen in the shadows behind the door. In any case, why should I bother about the man any further? My indignation withered away now that I'd relieved my feelings by telling him what I thought of him and his colleagues. To hell with the whole lot of them! Suddenly losing interest, I decided to waste no more time and walked out through the door, through the narrow opening into the street beyond, glad to be leaving the place behind me.

Like my feelings, it seemed to wither into unreality as I hurried along, conscious of nothing except the symptoms of my cold, which had been temporarily in abeyance but which now returned to burden me with heavy discomfort. Back at the flat I only remember thinking how many flights of stairs there were to be climbed laboriously. I'd even forgotten that Carla was coming.

She'd already let herself in and was waiting for me, reading by a single light. When I opened the door, not expecting to see her – not even thinking of her – the shock of her beauty took me unawares, like a revelation, waking me momentarily from my stupor. For an enchanted instant the old magic revived, and I eagerly started towards her.

I distinctly saw her stand up and come to meet me with a welcoming smile. There was no rational cause for my feeling that she receded as I approached, gliding away from me like an unattainable vision, too beautiful to be true. Nevertheless, the illusion seemed stronger than truth. My magic moment over, I stopped a short distance from her and stood still, relapsing into dull heaviness, as if not fully awake.

I heard her say, 'So you've been out?' in a questioning tone. But my head was aching so much I could think of no answer and simply stood staring. She had moved out of the circle of soft lamplight, and against the shadows her face appeared palely lit, mysterious as a miracle or a dream.

Her loveliness made me more aware of my ugly, heavy cold, which became exaggerated into something shameful. As if by contrast with her perfection, even my brain had grown ugly and stupid; its slow stupid thoughts didn't seem to belong to me. I felt altogether strange and unlike myself, a combination of shame and incapacity having replaced the person I really was, and this seemed to be her deliberate doing. Sudden resentment flared through my daze. Why should she make me ashamed of having a cold? Her beauty, which had charmed me the previous moment, had turned into a source of grievance. The memory of yesterday's unexplained painful events at her home thrust itself upon me, and a crowd of urgent questions clamoured for answers. 'Why did you leave me alone so long in the library? Had you arranged to meet that official? Who is he? Just how well do you know him? Why haven't you ever mentioned him to me?' Instead of any of these, I asked abruptly, 'Why are you in the dark?' at the same time switching on the strong centre light we hardly ever used.

This instinctive attempt to destroy her composure did not succeed, for, though the sudden light made her blink, she remained imperturbable as before. I had only exposed myself, and I stood revealed as a boorish, uncivilized lout to whom she would be eternally inaccessible.

Beginning to sink back hopelessly into stupefaction, to rouse myself I started pacing the room, deliberately working myself up to make a scene, determined to penetrate her calm. If I couldn't reach her, at least I would make her angry and bring her down nearer my own level. To concentrate on this was a fearful effort; my dull, estranged thoughts kept sliding away from me into blankness. But I stubbornly continued my pacing, persistently dwelling on the things I resented, as if with somebody else's brain, taking care not to look at Carla; who, realizing no doubt the futility of trying any reasonable approach while I was in this mood, kept silent and out of sight.

Presently I felt a faint itch of curiosity, wanting to know what she was doing. Stealing a furtive glance, I saw her bending over some frail wintry flowers she had brought, arranging them in a bowl on the table, her expression absorbed and withdrawn. Her cool, private self-sufficiency struck me as being assumed for the purpose of hurting and excluding me. Yet she seemed like some fabulous being at the same time, as if she wasn't quite human; an ice maiden, perhaps, intent on her delicate frost flowers and immune from our emotions.

A sudden monstrous desire to hurt her transfixed me; I wanted to assert my gross earthly condition over her ethereal otherness. What I experienced wasn't so much a wish as an uncontrollable upthrust of malice, springing from unexplored depths of my being – depths so strange and unsuspected that they seemed utterly alien, augmenting the disconcerting sense of estrangement from my own self. I couldn't bear this sense of a stranger's vindictiveness, it was torture to me but a torture incorporating a perverse satisfaction as when one intentionally bites on an aching tooth.

After the one quick glance, I hadn't looked at Carla again. But the flowers, directly under the light, caught and held my eyes and I stopped to stare at them. All at once it struck me that they were staring back; their pale, still, imperturbable faces were lifted to me in utter indifference, deputizing for the girl's face at which I would not look. This was the very last straw. The insult of those inhuman flower faces in league with her inhumanity against me was more than I could endure. I had to shut them out of my sight.

My hand began moving upwards to cover my eyes; then, with a weird sensation of abstract malice, I felt it shoot out suddenly in a different direction, like the hand of another person, crashing into something smooth and hard and sending it flying, while, above the noise of smashing china, I heard incoherent shouting. 'I can't stand the sight of those things – don't bring them into the place – so far and no further – it doesn't belong to you, and neither do I – yet.'

The excitement I'd been working so hard to raise surged over me and for a second swept me beyond myself. Gradually then it dawned on me that the cold-strangled voice with the ugly overtone of hysteria was my own; and with this realization the madness, delirium, or whatever it was, expired exactly as though it had never been, leaving only an incubus, a weight like a bad dream, from which I couldn't wake, pinning me down and dividing me from the world. As if I'd dropped asleep on my feet, I stood mute and inert, no more than an upright mass of dead matter, except for a single point of anxiety, buried very deep down, warning me of sensation to come, some time in the future.

Water, streaming over the table, cascaded on to the floor, carrying with it some of the scattered flowers, their fragile petals already bruised and crumpled. Without feeling I stared at the havoc I had created, unable to face the reality of what I'd done. It was as if my nerves had gone dead. There was the havoc, and the reality of it was there, like a man with his shadow, but the two wouldn't come together. I kept my eyes lowered, not wanting to see Carla. The thought, I must apologize, was in my head but, like everything else, rendered meaningless and cut off from me by the heaviness, as of sleep, which oppressed me.

She was the one who spoke first, asking me, with no trace of emotion, to stand aside, leaning over the table and wiping it with a cloth and, only when she'd cleared up the mess, confronting me very directly to say, 'Why don't you break off our engagement instead of trying to provoke me to do it for you?'

I heard the words and understood them; but the pressure of aching heaviness in my head kept their meaning apart, and, to my mind peering through curtains of strangeness, it seemed barely possible that an answer should be expected of me. All I could do was to raise my head, most laboriously as if heaving up some unwieldy great object, so that we came face to face. Her lovely paleness, untroubled-seeming as always, again reminded me of a snow maiden – cold, disheartening association – with large lustrous eyes looking at me darkly from far away. But, thought I – someone else's dull thoughts churning away in my dazed state – a snow maiden should have blue eyes or green, the colour of ice-shadows in a crevasse. Instead, there were these two dark crystals, very lovely and very strange. Was this *all* the strangeness I'd always seen in her face? Could the whole secret be merely that she had the wrong-coloured eyes?

The distracting question opened and shut ephemeral wings on the brink of the situation, where Carla, beautiful and unreal, awaited the answer I could not feel called upon to give.

Finally she spoke again. 'I've felt for some time that you didn't want to go on. But I hoped you'd be honest enough to tell me. However . . .'

The last word was scarcely more than a sigh. Still she watched, still expecting me to say something. Nothing suggested itself. What could I possibly say to a snow maiden? Her watchful eyes made me uneasy, and I started frantically searching my empty head, turning out every cupboard and dusty corner but only to find a few Latin phrases and names of schoolboys, unremembered for years. I was thankful when she relieved me of this fruitless quest for speech and slowly turned to the chair on which she'd left her outdoor things. I watched her move in bright, ethereal otherness among the ponderous down-to-earth shapes of the furniture, and my throat ached because she would soon be gone, back to whatever enchanted country she came from. But I did nothing to stop her going – that didn't seem to be in my power.

I felt utterly unfamiliar to myself, inextricably mixed up with headache and heaviness; and there was always that oppressiveness on me, like a waking sleep. The high room was so still I fancied that I could hear the tiny electric crackle of Carla's hair as she combed it; and somewhere a drop of water fell regularly as a clock ticking, marking the seconds, while everything seemed to wait in suspense as she went to the door.

At the last, at the open door, unbearably, she turned to look at me again, the dark landing behind her. I had no nerves, no emotions; I was asleep. And yet I couldn't stand it and quickly looked away. And when I looked back at the door she was no longer there. I saw only the dark empty space where she'd been standing, as if the darkness had taken her with a huge black, silent hand while I wasn't looking. All I heard was her light descending step on the stairs, receding from me, flight after flight, into the dark depths of the empty house; and, at the end, the final muted thump of the outer door.

My heart gave a great bound, and something went through me like lightning, like steel, that might have been either despair or triumph. It was all over. I had known all along. Now I'd achieved my object, the thing I most dreaded and most desired. I was alone again, unloving, unloved, as I always had been and would always be, world without end. At this moment of spontaneous revelation, the truth emerged, unmistakably, everywhere and in everything: shouted by the vast indifferent glacial silence of night and stars, petrified in the forever-suspended drop, proclaimed by the disposition of flowers, no longer scattered at random. For a timeless instant there was nothing but this hugely significant truth.

Then, slowly, I was aware of myself again, some tiresome detail of external reality would persist in molesting me, bringing me back to concrete things, to the light shining straight into my eyes. Mechanically, I moved a few steps out of the glare and, by making this automatic movement, fractured the spell. I couldn't return to where I had been. Slowly turning my head, I surveyed the room, which seemed both familiar and strange, like a room remembered from years ago. What had happened to me in this room? What had I been doing here?

Memory flooded back, and with it came a terrible black wave of desolation and loss; sweeping out of the dark building below, it towered over my head and exploded in soundless thunder, obliterating all thought, leaving only the urgent need to follow, to find – a need as elemental and all-excluding as the need for breath, displacing all other needs and thoughts.

I have no clear recollection of what came next, only of flying headlong from the house and of running, running, as if for dear life, stumbling and slipping in the icy streets, my footsteps shattering the stern nocturnal hush, seeing nothing, but all the time staring wildly about me, though whom I so frantically sought I didn't know. I have the impression that the streets were empty and that I met no one; but if they'd been crowded I probably wouldn't have noticed, so oblivious was I of everything but the one consuming need for a person without a name, without whom I couldn't live.

Somehow I must have got myself on to a bus, though I remember nothing about it except the conductor repeating, 'This is as far as we go', and looking at me very strangely. He must have said it several times already, for he shouted the words, doubtless thinking I was deaf, and when even then I didn't immediately understand him he glared at me fiercely, as if he suspected me of playing some trick on him, shaking my shoulder to get rid of me or wake me up. Horrified by the grasp of his large hand, which half recalled to me something that fearfully threatened, I jumped up and off the bus. But, once on the pavement, I had enough presence of mind to remember to walk slowly till I was out of his sight, only when I got around the corner starting to race away, with no thought for where I was going.

When breathlessness and a sharp, stabbing pain with each breath made me slow down, I didn't recognize my surroundings. The buildings seemed to have drawn back haughtily from the street, which trailed off into obscurity in the distance. Beside me a high brick wall rose perpendicular and unbroken by doors or windows, indeterminate black masses looming beyond; but it didn't dawn on me that I'd reached a suburb till I made out the bare skeleton of a tree. The odd thing was that, though I didn't know where I was, I instinctively turned in at an entrance gate and unhesitatingly passed through into the dark drive without pausing to wonder why, at this hour of the night, the gate should have been standing wide open.

The house was all in darkness, except for two lighted windows flanking the pillared porch, tall pointed windows I must have noticed without being aware of it on Christmas Day, for I remembered them now. It was, of course, Carla's home to which I'd been brought, as if by a will quite separate from my own. As I looked at it, the curtain of one of these windows was pulled aside, and with a kind of inevitability Carla herself appeared and stood looking out with an expectant air.

I was startled, for she seemed to be looking straight at me, and I hurriedly stepped aside, into a bank at the edge of the drive, up which I scrambled. Safely out of sight at the top, I could still see her peering out, as though she knew I was there somewhere in the darkness but with an odd uncertainty most unlike her usual steady gaze. For a second I couldn't focus the memory it recalled; and then my mother's image appeared so vividly that I could almost hear my own unkind boy's laughter mocking her superstition, and caught an instantaneous glimpse of similar resentful motives for my recent bad conduct. This backward flash over, I found myself thinking, even in my muddled state, that since Carla presumably was the person I'd been chasing with such urgency, I should have attracted her notice instead of avoiding it. But I had no real comprehension of my own acts or of anything else. And now her face was no longer clear. I couldn't even be sure that I'd really seen her at the window. This uncertainty, I realized, was entirely down to mental confusion. Something seemed to be wrong with my eyes, which I was continually rubbing as if wiping away tears, and it came back to me that for some time as I hurried along I'd been trying to clear my vision in this way.

Looking up now, I was astonished to see a great flock of small white birds descending on me, filling the air, gliding and hovering all about me, so close their cold wing-tips brushed my cheeks and forehead. I waved my arms to scare them away. But they came at me still more thickly, hiding the window and diving and darting right into my face as if to peck out my eyes and blind me altogether. When I saw that they weren't birds at all but great snowflakes I watched them, fascinated, as I'd always been in my child-hood, by their ceaseless falling and turning, a palely glisten-ing curtain that drifted down without end or beginning, lightly shaken from time to time by some wandering air cur-rent as it changed direction and sent small eddies scurrying to and fro.

Suddenly, startlingly, two level beams came swinging around from the street, drove purposefully through the glimmering stuff and pointed straight at the house, light-ing it up, though I myself was passed over and left to merge indistinguishably with the anonymous dark. In that setting, where all was vague, fluctuating and tenuous, these twin beams seemed, to my equally vague state of mind, to show an almost concrete definition and purpose, driving right to the heart of the situation, which was my rejection, while brightly illuminating what was forbidden to me.

I saw that they came from the headlights of a big car that had silently stopped just below me. And, instantly, I was transported to quite another time and place, gazing down with a child's awed astonishment at the great black beetle filling the width of the lane; then, aware of the weight of my rifle, watching the miraculous-seeming arrival at the foot of the school boundary wall.

These backward excursions confused my already uncertain identity even more. How could I be sure who I really was? To make the confusion worse, another picture now came before me, perhaps the memory of a dream, perhaps originating in some actual scene from the past, but transposed into a different dimension, where the face of apparent reality seemed about to drop, like a mask, to reveal the unimaginable strangeness behind. I was walking along the water's edge on an interminable beach of pale sand, following someone's footprints, which the small colourless waves were forever obliterating, though not so thoroughly that I ever lost sight of them ahead between the smooth, untrodden ellipses left by the water. Except for myself, the beach was absolutely forsaken, the sea on one side, and on the other walled in by high unscalable dunes. It seemed to have no end, and there was no escape from it, under the pale, tight-fitting lid of sky.

Though the powerful beams of the headlights recalled me instantly from this vision, it interfered for a moment with my view of the car and the snowstorm and Carla, standing in the porch, so asserting its uncomprehended significance. But before I could even ask myself what it meant, the sequence of events it had interrupted was once more restored. History seemed to be repeating itself when Spector emerged from the car into the white whirling dance of the snowflakes, which the light, spreading up, thickened into a falling fabric over his head, a faintly shimmering canopy.

Reverting to those two occasions my memory had retained so distinctly, I now felt the same shock, his presence seemed to assert itself with the same stark vividness, in the same abruptly portentous fashion. I only saw his face for a second before he turned to the girl, turning his back on me as if to confirm my rejection, so that I saw him as I had on Christmas Day and knew I'd recognized him even then.

So acutely was I conscious of him that when he took Carla's arm to lead her back indoors I felt his dominant possessiveness and his insistent will, as though it were *my* arm he was holding. My eyes confused by the shifting pattern of snowflakes, and my mind by the weirdly shifting flux of personalities and unstable time, I couldn't locate myself anywhere in my life. I couldn't understand the strange blend of nostalgia and resentment that filled me until, for the second time, my mother's image appeared, and I wanted to rush to Carla and pull her back, out of the tranquillity of her daydreaming face, because of my dream of the past, which ended so catastrophically.

My own dream was already ended, and that I was to have no part in hers was made clear by the way she and her companion were briefly outlined against the bright oblong of the open door, so closely joined by their linked arms that they might have been one. Despairing loneliness overwhelmed me as the door closed behind this composite figure of my two loves, now mysteriously become one and the same, excluding me with such decisive finality that I could only submit, as to a sentence passed on me long ago.

The lights went out. I felt at the same time a shift in my situation and that I'd been delivered into the power of my past. For a moment that seemed eternal I stood there, balanced precariously, high up in the darkness, bewildered by the unstable pallor forever falling out of a black sky, coldly, ghostlily, touching me and dissolving and touching again.

Somehow my surroundings were changing. I was afraid. It was dangerous for me to stay here, yet I dared not stir, pits of nothingness opening on every side. The world was dissolving in darkness and danger. Nothing was solid or safe any more in this high, unstable place, where a wan paleness wavered and fell like light through dense wind-shaken foliage. The very foundations of reality had begun to dissolve. I didn't know where I was, either in space or in my existence. Lost in the deepest possible sense, I'd lost even the reality of my life in the world. My real self was dissolving, falling away from me. To my horror I felt myself some small, despised, abject thing – some kind of vermin – without teeth or claws or any means of protection, the most defenceless creature alive, hated and hunted by all the rest. My destruction was their common duty, an easy task, accomplished by one weak blow.

Utterly vulnerable, at the mercy of the whole world, I was waiting alone in this high, rocking insecurity – from which I already seemed to have watched myself deserted by all I had once trusted – for the vengeance racing towards me out of the past. In full cry, the past was hunting me down, and I knew myself now eternally doomed and hated, a criminal, outcast, isolated by guilt from all other living things, rejected by life itself. There could be no expiation and no escape, except by the door into senseless blackness through which I had once sent –

As a nightmare breaks before the falling dreamer can hit the ground, before the past could swoop down on me, completing the memory, the situation shifted again. I was once more myself, though confused and diminished far beyond rational thought by the dreadful and dream-like strangeness of these latest experiences, which my sense of reality could barely survive.

My memory of what followed has always remained unclear. I have only a vague impression of reeling away from that place and afterwards of walking endlessly through the falling snow, which obscured the atmosphere and smothered the town in unnatural silence, its huge flakes swarming around the lights, which at long intervals punctuated the empty street, stretching ahead of me to infinity.

I remember how from time to time the pale, undulating veil parted and buildings, hugely distorted, loomed up like skyscrapers and how the white carpet, always thickening under foot, hid the edges of the pavement but would not bear my weight, so that I stumbled often and almost fell. I had the idea that the paving stones grew all the time larger, so that if I could have seen them I wouldn't have been able to stride from one to the next. I know I was dead tired and moved very slowly with the great effort of every step. And it seemed I would never arrive anywhere but must go on for ever like this, through the interminable, purgatorial, snowy streets, till at last I dropped from exhaustion. It would be very pleasant, I thought, to lie down on the untrodden white and let the snow cover me and hide my guilt out of sight; and I remember thinking how I'd pull this coverlet over my head, as I used to pull up the bedclothes when I was a child and wanted to hide from some disappointment or shame. But for some reason it wasn't allowed now, and I had to keep moving, alone as surely I'd never been before, in the silent cold night, irremediably forsaken, all warmth, all affection, everything I had loved and trusted withdrawn from me absolutely and for all time.

What comes back to me when I think about it is a childish loneliness and forlornness, growing gradually into that feeling of being lost and internally cold that used to bewilder me during the hard winter of my mother's indifference long ago, when I piled logs on the fires but could light no corresponding warmth in her heart or my own. It was only the cold inside me of which I was conscious; I don't recollect feeling cold in my body, though I'd been so long in the snow without the overcoat that I had, of course, forgotten when I rushed out of the flat. I suppose I was feverish and indebted to fever for this resurgence of those old feelings of deprivation and frustrated love that I substituted for others less bearable, which should have been my concern. At all events, I was ill after this and ran a high temperature for several days.

How I eventually got home I don't know; nor do I know how or why the caretaker's wife came to appoint herself my nurse, for she neither asked nor volunteered anything and indeed rarely spoke to me at all. Until now I'd only been vaguely aware of this strange, silent woman, who never spoke to anyone as she went in or out of the building and always wore the same blank, discouraging face; but now I was glad she was looking after me, for she wouldn't gossip, I knew, about anything I might let slip while the fever was at its height.

Throughout this period my guilt pursued me relentlessly, evidence of it appearing frequently in my surroundings, convincing me that I was directly responsible for my parents' deaths. If I had really planned the double murder in cold blood I could hardly have experienced greater torments of distress and self-loathing than those I suffered in the hallucinatory fever world, where images from the past mingled confusingly in my head with more recent memories.

Wherever I looked, I saw reminders of my crime. The

harmless ceiling geography of cracks and stains changed before my eyes into the disastrous mushroom shape of explosion, spouting horrid details, fragments of limbs and clothing. If my gaze fixed itself on the bedspread, the oriental design would soon become a sort of exotic jungle, out of which sneering, sub-human faces would peer, reminiscent of the sinister chessmen at school.

My only respite from guilt was when Carla seemed to be in the room, very lovely, her hair darkly framing her calm pale face; but this was almost as bad, for her serene shining gaze was always cold and indifferent. She never smiled, never spoke to me nor touched me. And though she some-times leaned over the bed as though to kiss me, I came to dread this more than anything, because of the way her face always became distorted as it approached mine, vanishing at last with a look of disgust or a mocking smile it had never worn in real life.

Spector, too, made his appearance, a tall, shadowy, menacing figure, faceless and almost formless, towering above me in mysterious silent denunciation. And some-times the two of them would seem to blend into each other as they had done in the porch, so that I couldn't tell whether one or both kept watch on me from the shadows gathered thickly under the sloping ceilings.

These visitations left so strong an impression that after-wards it was hard for me to believe neither of the people concerned had really been there; which accounted, I think, for my failure – when my temperature fell and the delusions left me – to appreciate the completeness of the break between us. Without consciously thinking about it, I must have assumed that sooner or later one or other of them would reappear and reclaim me, otherwise I couldn't have been so calm – I couldn't have given way to the profound lethargy that for some time made me indifferent to everything. Long after I became convalescent and was, physically, on the road to recovery, my mental state remained unchanged. I couldn't bear the prospect of taking up my life in the world again. At the same time, it was impossible for me not to realize that there was something distinctly abnormal, not to be accounted for by my short illness, about an apathy so deep and prolonged. The mere thought of resuming my former activities was abhorrent to me. And, fascinated, almost, by this heavy torpor, I began to explore it and to write down what I found, thus occupying many long, solitary hours of my convalescence.

It was obvious that, to get at the truth, I would have to delve back into my early memories, as I've tried to do here. At first I was troubled by Spector's over-prominence in the picture, emerging from the start as a huge, isolated, out-of-scale figure, obscuring and falsifying the rest. But his significance always was out of proportion, and I should have been falsifying the scene had I made less of it. And I soon perceived that his influence over me had not really diminished, as, sensing its opposition to my love affair, I'd pretended it had. A secret interior conflict had, in fact, reduced me to my present state, the two conflicting loyalties, which had been tugging in opposite directions till I was practically pulled in half, having ended by immobilizing me altogether.

My investigations had led to a reassessing of intellectual values, and I saw that, though my conclusion was accurate as far as it went, it was not the whole truth. As soon as I decided I'd have to dig down still deeper to uncover the root of my listless withdrawal from life, I became aware of some interference from the past distracting and confusing my thoughts, causing me a sensation that was at the same time oppressive, expectant and empty. In these somewhat contradictory feelings, I came to recognize my childish sense of having run down like a clock that needed someone to wind it before it could go again; and saw that I was now no less helpless than in those far-off days when I waited for somebody to take me by the hand and tell me what to do. On my own initiative I could do nothing, take no responsibility, make no decisions only watch my existence unroll.

All my life I'd been dependent on a stronger personality and had accepted the principle of my dependence so thoroughly that I regarded it as inevitable, and was waiting now as passively as a silver cup on its plinth for either Carla or Spector to claim me, not even very much caring which of them dominated me again.

The ambivalence that had always made me unsure whether I loved the man more than I hated and feared him, or vice versa, now extended to the girl as well. Carla's beauty, I knew, would always have power to charm me, but whether I still loved her I very much doubted. It was with her that I had experienced my most intense happiness. But now, thinking about her, I had a double impression, a memory of past joy and of more recent mistrust and resentment. Incidents she had never explained had left me with an unhealed wound and the suspicion that both she and Spector had been making use of me for their own unknown personal ends.

Against my will, the picture I always tried to forget formed in front of me with such detailed distinctness that I really seemed to be watching all over again the two enlaced figures going into the house, joined as closely as one. With my own eyes I had witnessed their intimacy – there was no getting around it. Now, suddenly, my new respect for truth asserted itself. I found I could no longer go on deluding myself with the idea that one or other of them was bound to take possession of me, as in the past. For the first time since my illness I felt disturbed. Uneasiness pervading my lethargy, I got up and started restlessly pacing the room. If I was not to lead the old life of dependence, what *was* my future life to be?

I stopped and looked out of the window. The last faint tinge of a stormy sunset still smouldered in the sky above, but down in the streets it was already night and the lamps had been lit. The time of the evening rush had begun, and from this height the crowds surging in every direction seemed to move with the aimless chaotic frenzy of disturbed insects. The sight troubled me obscurely, and I drew the curtains sharply across the window to shut it out.

Most emphatically, I did not want to be one of the scurrying, nameless thousands down there. This thought led to another slight shock, as I remembered how I'd once taken a pride in being indistinguishable from the people around me. But this only seemed to prove my fundamental difference, I now thought, for surely, if I'd really been like everyone else, such an extraordinary notion would never have entered my head. I'd have taken the similarity for granted.

So in reality I'd never been the confident, normal young man of my thoughts at all. Logically following upon this conviction came the equally disconcerting corollary: I had never been a schoolboy either, or a lover, or any of the various beings I'd impersonated at various stages of my career.

I should have liked to put an end to these thoughts, by which I was becoming more and more disturbed, but they seemed to crowd into my head independently and against my will. I had the feeling that enlightenment was pressing so hard upon me that it created a sense of danger – but I could do nothing about it, and, though I was afraid of where my thoughts might lead, I had to follow them along the path they had chosen.

I'd never been anything but 'in transit' through my life. In a sudden, complete, instantaneous vision, I saw it as a train and myself as a passenger always changing compartments, moving on to another before getting to know the self left behind in the last carriage. I'd always presumed these old outgrown personalities had ceased to exist when I discarded them, possibly lingering on for a while as remembered ghosts of what they had been, till they finally sank into oblivion, dead and forgotten. Now, for the first time, I understood that it wasn't possible to discard any part of myself. Seeing all these unknown selves sitting where I'd left them, staring out of the windows through the eyes I'd once shared, I was struck most forcibly by the fact that I hadn't got rid of them after all; they were still in the same train with me and always would be as long as I travelled in it. This meant that at any time any one of them was liable to spring out of his place, chase me along the corridor to my present compartment and there take possession of me, temporarily directing my actions and supplanting my current self.

It was an alarming thought that these false selves should still have me in their power, and in my bewilderment I began wondering whether any such thing as my real self could be said to exist at all. Like a sudden revelation, then, it became clear to me that the self was always changing, always developing, only capable of evolving fully through the integration of all past semblances. I wouldn't be my true self till I accepted and learned to know all those selves I'd disowned and deserted.

As if this were something I could do consciously, there and then, the last of my inertia vanished, consumed by an ardent desire for identification with the essential 'I' – until this had been achieved I'd always be as I was now, wandering like a stranger, lost, frightened and confused, among the changes and contradictions of my own personality.

Since I wrote those last words some days have passed; days as empty as all the days of my convalescence, though filled for me by the slow inward crystallization of a momentous decision. In pursuing my lassitude to its source I have overcome it, learning in the process something about myself – only a very little, yet enough to grasp the vital necessity of self-knowledge. Now, at least, I'm aware of what I must already have known subconsciously when I renounced companionship and the chance of contentment for the elusive ghost I hope will one day be closer to me than a brother. Often I seem to feel his nearness, though he always keeps out of sight. Sometimes I've fancied he was hovering just behind me, but however quickly I turn he still evades me, gliding through doors and walls like my old friend the tall, thin man. The atmosphere of this flat must be saturated by the double influence of the two strong characters who have both frequented it, with me and in my absence. And it's because instinct tells me outside influences keep us apart, so that I can't expect him to meet me here, that I've decided to go away. It's been a terribly difficult decision for me; but I'm convinced I'll only attain my object when I've left this place far behind me.

Though I'm so eager to meet this being composed of all my past selves, the prospect frightens me, too. I'm afraid of the face I and other people may have given him or, worst of all, that he may be faceless. Once in imagination – or was it in reality? – I felt my inmost self dissolve and fall away from me. And lately I've developed a foolish trick of looking the other way when I pass a mirror, in case there should be no reflection there. To find that the personality I've been building up all my life was without a face would be the most appalling of all possible discoveries.

I'm quite prepared to meet the face of a criminal. I've known guilt all my life and been shunned and hated for it by my fellow creatures. In a sense, guilt has evolved me; without it, neither I nor my other self could exist. Not only is that self the criminal but the victim as well, the judge and, ultimately, the executioner. I can accept my guilt now that I recognize it as my own creation. We all of us construct our own worlds from what is within us, and this is the obvious reason why it's so vitally important to know what is there.

When others only exist as we choose to see them, it becomes futile to apportion blame, so to say Spector damaged me irreparably has no meaning. Evidently I needed to be injured in precisely this way, and if he hadn't inflicted the injury I'd have forced someone else to do it. Indeed, I sometimes think I've imagined both him and Carla and created their joint behaviour as a punishment for my guilt. The image of their closely joined bodies has printed itself indelibly on my brain, so that I often now see them as one person, of whom I'm afraid; for I can never escape them if they are projections of my own personality.

But my resolve remains fixed and unshakeable. I can't stay here in their ambience any longer. My bag is packed; in an hour or so I'll be gone. Of course, if he wishes, Spector will find me quite easily. But why should he bother to persecute me, if I retire to the remote countryside to live the life of a recluse? Perhaps in time he will let me forget him, and his immense black shadow, which has darkened my whole existence, will fade at last. Already his image seems less formidable, as I see in it only the calamities I have wished myself.

As for Carla, if she has any separate identity in the concrete world, I can only hope to meet her again some time in the future when all this is forgotten and there is no need of deceit or misunderstanding. How easy it is to deceive trusting people with lies. But I must have required her to deceive me, and I'm no longer resentful, nor am I so unreasonable as to complain.

It all began, probably, with my trying to live in the city; that was my great mistake, for I've never felt my natural self when surrounded by crowds and buildings. Perhaps I'll have a better chance of leading my own life in solitude, among the hills and valleys and woods where I was born and grew up. To understand the self is all that matters, and then all things become possible; perhaps there, in the neighbourhood where the crime was committed, I may even come to terms with my guilt.

In an hour or so I shall go to the station, take the first train to the part of the country where I used to live, getting out wherever it happens to stop, leaving everything to chance or, rather, following my instincts, prepared to accept whatever circumstances ensue. There's a certain comfort at times like these in abandoning all conscious effort to control one's destiny, and so I am making no plans. My suitcase is packed with only the barest necessities, for this period of my life is over, and I want to carry forward as little of it as possible into the next. A new beginning implies a new world as well as the end of an old one; in the depths of the country I may perhaps rediscover that mysterious sanctuary where I once used to take refuge from the world of facts and the harshness and misunderstanding I found among human beings.

'That's nothing but cowardly defeatism,' I seem to hear some disapproving critic exclaim. 'You're just running away from life and from your problems.' And I answer that this can't be so, for the simple reason that it's impossible to run away from what is within one. Granted, I may only be at the beginning of greater problems and difficulties; but at any rate I shall know that they are of my own making and not down to alien influence.

I wonder whether I've made it sound too easy, this course I am taking. Anybody who's ever attempted to do it will know that it's never easy to start life again, especially with very little money and without friends. Eternal regret is the price I must pay for the idyllic companionship I have known and lost. Now I'm more alone than I've ever been, not only because I no longer have any friends but because I know that, however closely another life may impinge upon mine, ultimately I exist in impenetrable isolation.

So I come to the end of my writing. I've often thought it was of no value, my ideas of no more significance than the aimless circling of flies in an empty room. And, if anyone else ever reads these words, he'll probably endorse this opinion, saying these are trivial personal matters that tell him nothing he didn't already know.

To such a person I must admit that I deserve his criticism, for communication was not my primary object. But my egotism seems justified by the understanding, to which the writing has led, of things that are of supreme importance to me, though possibly they are incommunicable.

Also by Anna Kavan and available from Peter Owen

Ice

ISBN 978 0 7206 1268 4

£9.95

'There is nothing else like it . . . This *Ice* is not psychological ice or metaphysical ice; here the loneliness of childhood has been magicked into a physical reality as hallucinatory as the Ancient Mariner's.'
– Doris Lessing

In this haunting and surreal novel, the narrator and a man known as 'the warden' search for an elusive girl in a frozen, seemingly post-nuclear, apocalyptic landscape. The country has been invaded and is being governed by a secret organization. There is destruction everywhere; great walls of ice overrun the world. Together with the narrator, the reader is swept into a hallucinatory quest for this strange and fragile creature with albino hair. Acclaimed by Brian Aldiss on its publication in 1967 as the best science fiction book of the year, this extraordinary and innovative novel has subsequently been recognized as a major work of literature in any genre.

'A classic, a vision of unremitting intensity which combines some remarkable imaginative writing with what amounts to a love-song to the end of the world. Not a word is wasted, not an image is out of place.'
– *Times Literary Supplement*

'One of the most mysterious of modern writers, Anna Kavan created a uniquely fascinating fictional world. Few contemporary novelists could match the intensity of her vision.' – J.G. Ballard

'One of the most terrifying postulations about the end of the world . . . one can only admire the strength and courage of this visionary.' – *The Times*

Peter Owen books can be purchased from: Central Books, 99 Wallis Road, London E9 5LN, UK
Tel: + 44 (0)20 8986 4854 Fax: + 44 (0)20 8533 5821 e-mail: orders@centralbooks.com

Also by Anna Kavan and available from Peter Owen

Asylum Piece

ISBN 978 0 7206 1123 6

£9.95

'If only one knew of what and by whom one were accused, when, where and by what laws one were to be judged, it would be possible to prepare one's defence systematically and set about things in a sensible fashion.'
— Anna Kavan, *Asylum Piece*

First published sixty years ago, *Asylum Piece* today ranks as one of the most extraordinary and terrifying evocations of human madness ever written. This collection of stories, mostly interlinked and largely autobiographical, chart the descent of the narrator from the onset of neurosis to final incarceration in a Swiss clinic. The sense of paranoia, of persecution by a foe or force that is never given a name, evokes *The Trial* by Franz Kafka, the writer with whom Kavan is most often compared, although Kavan's deeply personal, restrained and almost foreign-accented style has no true model. The same characters who recur throughout — the protagonist's unhelpful 'adviser', the friend/lover who abandons her at the clinic and an assortment of deluded companions — are sketched without a trace of the rage, self-pity or sentiment that have marked many other accounts of mental instability.

'Pervaded by a sense of intolerable oppression, lit by sudden shafts of delight in the natural world, their concise artistry proclaims how consummately she knew and rode her devils.' – *Guardian*
'Anna Kavan charges the space between her words and the reader's mind with a continuous crackle of electricity.' – *New Statesman*
'A classic equal to the work of Kafka.' – Anaïs Nin

Peter Owen books can be purchased from: Central Books, 99 Wallis Road, London E9 5LN, UK
Tel: + 44 (0)20 8986 4854 Fax: + 44 (0)20 8533 5821 e-mail: orders@centralbooks.com

Also available from Peter Owen

A Stranger on Earth:
The Life and Work of Anna Kavan
Jeremy Reed

ISBN 978 0 7206 1273 8

£13.99

A Stranger on Earth documents Kavan's lifelong addiction to heroin, the circumstances of her two failed marriages, the inseparable bond she formed with her psychiatrist, her suicide attempts, her strange and unforgettable paintings, her devoted attraction to gay men, her obsessions, phobias, reclusiveness and indomitable artistic courage. Reed also celebrates the extraordinary imagination at work in her highly acclaimed novels, such as *Asylum Piece*, *Sleep Has His House*, *Ice* and *Mercury*. Admirers include J.G. Ballard, Doris Lessing, Brian Aldiss and Anaïs Nin, and her work has influenced a generation of younger writers, from Elizabeth Wurtzel to Will Self.

'This superb biography peels back the mysteries that surround one of the strangest writers of the twentieth century. The brilliance of Anna Kavan lay somewhere between poetry and madness, and Jeremy Reed takes us deep into the heart of this extraordinary woman. A gripping intellectual thriller.' – J.G. Ballard

'Anna Kavan, with her frightening glimpses of the dark sides of life, is one of the world's best-kept secrets. Her extraordinary life deserves this fascinating biography.' – Virginia Ironside

ooks can be purchased from: Central Books, 99 Wallis Road, London E9 5LN, UK
20 8986 4854 Fax: + 44 (0)20 8533 5821 e-mail: orders@centralbooks.com